Freya's GOLD

FIONA LONGMUIR

nosy crow

First published in the UK in 2024 by Nosy Crow Ltd
Wheat Wharf, 27a Shad Thames,
London, SE1 2XZ, UK

Nosy Crow Eireann Ltd
44 Orchard Grove, Kenmare,
Co Kerry, V93 FY22, Ireland

Nosy Crow and associated logos are trademarks and/or registered
trademarks of Nosy Crow Ltd

ISBN: 978 1 80513 097 0

A CIP catalogue record for this book is available from the
British Library.

Printed and bound in the UK by Clays Ltd, Elcograf S.p.A.
following rigorous ethical sourcing standards.
Typeset by Tiger Media

Papers used by Nosy Crow are made from wood grown in
sustainable forests

MIX
Paper | Supporting
responsible forestry
FSC® C018072

1 3 5 7 9 10 8 6 4 2

www.nosycrow.com

For Niall,
who holds up the world
so I can create new ones.

One

In summer the Bright and Breezy B&B lived up to its name. The rocky beach out front glimmered with tiny pools, falling gradually away to the golden curve of the sandy beach on the other side of Edge. The horizon was bookended by the glint of the lighthouse on one side and the craggy black face of the cliffs on the other. With only the wooden planks of the old boardwalk between its front door and the beach, the B&B offered views of the sparkling sea from almost every room. More importantly it also offered the best cooked breakfast in town.

In summer the B&B buzzed with families and holidaymakers, who travelled from the city to stretch out on the warm sand and breathe the fresh sea air. It became a living, breathing thing, crammed with battered suitcases and sandy babies and sunburnt noses.

Freya liked living in the B&B with her Granny Kate in summer, liked sweeping floors and washing dishes to earn a bit of pocket money. Most of all she liked the travellers who came to the B&B with stories of far-off places and grand adventures. At twelve she had never been further than the neighbouring city. Even when her parents were alive, they'd lived only a few streets away. Visitors would smile warmly at her and tell her how lucky she was to live in such a beautiful place, what a picturesque life she must lead.

"Yes," she'd tell them, silently adding *in summer*.

Freya loved Edge in summer, but it always felt like a trick. It was like a little kid in its Sunday best, sitting up straight and smiling angelically at the grown-ups. As the days started to shorten and the holidaymakers drifted back to the city, Freya knew a whole other Edge was on the way. The breeziness of the B&B turned frigid. The wind flew down narrow streets, rattling shutters and tweaking mischievously at noses and scarves. It whipped the sea into frenzied foam, coating the town in freezing sticky salt. Clouds sat heavy in the sky and some days it felt like the sun didn't bother to rise at all. No one came to Edge in the off season.

The transformation always made Freya uneasy. It felt like proof that even the loveliest things were hiding something dark and secret. Edge turned eerie and strange, full of looming silences and shadowy corners. And Freya's imagination always seemed to fill those corners with something terrible. She wondered what the smiling tourists would make of Edge in February.

She shivered despite the fire roaring in the grate beside her. She was perched at the reception desk of the B&B because it was the warmest place in the building. The sleety rain that had soaked her on the way home from school battered against the windows. Her coat was slung over the chair in front of the fire, steaming as it dried. She curled her toes further into the fluffy belly of Sir Lancelot, the B&B's enormous orange cat.

She swiped at her foggy glasses and tried to focus on the pile of maths homework in front of her. But her attention was snagged by the ticking of the clock on the desk. She'd been thinking about building an alarm clock but wasn't sure how to go about it. She sneaked a look behind her to check that Granny Kate was nowhere to be seen, picked up the clock and popped off the back. The inside of the clock was alive with whirring cogs and wheels. Warmth spread through Freya all the way to her fingertips. It never failed to amaze her that something as simple as a clock could contain this whole world of moving parts. She sat very still, watching the pieces turn. She was so absorbed that she almost toppled clean off her chair when the door to the B&B was flung open.

A tall dark shape filled the door, and Freya's brain instinctively yelled, *Monster!* In February that seemed about as likely as a person arriving. But as the figure stepped through the door and pulled it closed behind them, Freya saw that it *was* a person. A woman. She was tall and was wearing a long green coat that swished behind her as she moved. The hem was dark where it had dragged along the wet ground. The woman moved like a dancer, seemingly unbothered by the huge suitcase in her hand or the fact that she was soaked to the skin. She glided towards Freya, baring a mouthful of even white teeth as she approached the desk. The cold was coming off her in waves and goosebumps raced across Freya's skin. Sir Lancelot wriggled out from under Freya's feet and hopped up on to the desk to hiss at the stranger. Freya pushed him out of the way with difficulty.

She almost asked "Are you lost?" but in the end settled for "Can I help you?"

"Goodness me," said the woman. "Receptionists are getting younger every day."

Freya placed a polite smile on her face. Why did grown-ups think that joke was funny?

"My Granny Kate runs the place," she said. "I'm Freya."

"Freya! What a beautiful name."

"I guess."

She reached for the bell. The woman gestured at the pile of maths books on the desk. "That looks dreadful."

Freya shrugged. "I like maths."

"Oh. Then lucky you."

An awkward silence fell. Freya pressed the bell. From the next room there was the distinct sound of someone heaving themselves out of an armchair.

"Freya, if I have to tell you one more time about playing with that bell –"

Granny Kate stopped as she spotted the woman in front of the desk. Judging by the fact that her hair was pinned in pink rollers, she hadn't been expecting anyone either. She pursed her lips and visibly decided to style it out. She drew herself up to her full height, which was still absolutely tiny. "Can I help you, dear?"

"I was wondering if it would be possible to check in."

Freya's head jerked up. "Here?"

The woman laughed, the sound like a teaspoon tinkling in a cup. "Do people often arrive looking to check in elsewhere?"

"Oh. No. They don't often arrive looking to check in in February at all."

Granny Kate stepped pointedly in front of Freya. "What my granddaughter means to say is that you're very welcome. I'm Kate Lawson and I run the B&B. And you've met Freya already. Can I take your name, please?"

"Vivien Oleander."

Granny Kate pulled out the visitor book and started to take down Ms Oleander's details. Freya took the opportunity to study her more closely. She was elegantly dressed despite the wild weather. Her hair was gathered and pinned on one side with an enamel clasp, spilling over her shoulder. Neat square fingernails drummed gently on the desk. She didn't look much like their usual visitors.

Freya glanced at Ms Oleander's name in the visitor book, the only one on the page. She was their first guest of the year, and the first for quite some time before that. Freya knew that Granny Kate worried during the winter, when bills were high and there were no guests.

She supposed she should make an effort. "Are you on your holidays then?"

The woman's smile stretched further. "Something like that."

"Something like that?"

"Freya, hush," said Granny Kate. "And how long are you planning to stay with us, Ms Oleander?"

"Two weeks at least."

Freya frowned. "You don't know how long you're on your holidays for?"

"Freya," said Granny Kate, and there was an edge in her voice now, "would you throw another log on? The fire is looking a little low."

It wasn't, and Freya opened her mouth to say so, but Granny Kate fixed her with a death stare. She sighed as loudly as she dared, which wasn't very loudly, and slid round the desk. She watched as the woman slipped a bundle of crisp notes out of her purse and handed them across the desk to Granny Kate.

Granny Kate counted them briskly and wrote out

a receipt for two weeks' stay. "Breakfast is served in the room to your right. You're our only guest at the moment, so if you let me know what time you want it, I can have it ready for you."

"I'm an early riser."

Freya shuddered. *A morning person.*

Granny Kate gave a curt, approving nod. "Very good. Eight?"

"Perfect."

"Any allergies?"

"Just penicillin."

"Don't worry, that doesn't feature on our menu," said Granny Kate, returning the visitor book to its drawer.

Ms Oleander's eyes swept the reception as Granny Kate disappeared behind the desk. She almost looked hungry as she took it all in. Maybe she was thinking about breakfast. But somehow Freya didn't think so. Something about those bright, hungry eyes made the skin on Freya's neck start to creep. Her imagination began to colour Ms Oleander as a monster again, ready to swallow the B&B whole the second Freya turned away. Freya pressed her back against the wall, keeping her eyes fixed on Ms Oleander. She pictured the woman as a jewelled green dragon, and saw herself with a sword in her hand valiantly protecting her home.

"And you'll have your pick of the rooms, of course," said Granny Kate.

"Room Three has the best view!" Freya chirped.

The death stare returned. "All the rooms have the same view," said Granny Kate.

Freya wracked her brain. What did grown-ups care about? "And the best … shower?"

"Freya! Stop badgering Ms Oleander!"

Ms Oleander shook her head. "That's quite all right. Room Three sounds perfect, thank you."

Granny Kate plucked the key from the board behind her and tossed it to Freya.

"Why don't you hang up that wet coat and come through to the breakfast room for a cup of tea? I've got a fire going in there already, so it's nice and warm. Freya can take your case to your room."

Ms Oleander's knuckles tightened on the handle of

her case but she turned and set it down in front of Freya. "That's so kind, thank you."

Freya picked it up, trying not to wince at the weight. She hefted it against one hip and bumped her way through the doors on the far side of the reception. It was slow going. The case was excruciatingly heavy and the stairs were narrow and twisting. At one point Freya found herself wedged between the suitcase and the wall and had to give it a good kick to get it moving again. She hoped Ms Oleander didn't notice. She almost regretted not suggesting a room on the ground floor.

After what felt like an eternity she shoved her way through the door of Room Three. She dropped the case with a thud and leaned against the door, breathing heavily. Sweat cooled on her skin, making her shiver. She eyed the suitcase. It was one of those big old-fashioned ones. Brown leather with two enormous buckles and a large combination lock. There was a luggage tag attached to the handle but it didn't say anything.

She poked the case with her toe. Maybe she could

just have a quick peek inside. She could always say she was trying to be helpful and get Ms Oleander unpacked. She thought of the way Ms Oleander's hand had tightened on the handle. Maybe not. Besides, she wasn't nosy. Not really. She shoved the case over by the bed and turned back towards the door. She glanced down at the vent in the wall. The one that fed through to her room on the floor below. Total coincidence, of course. She'd completely forgotten it was there.

Two

Freya was woken the next morning by the sound of rain hammering against her bedroom window. Not quite ready to face the cold, she dragged her duvet over to her desk, picked up the clock from reception and took it back to her bed. She turned it over in her hands, tugging at a large cog with her fingernail. Trying to keep the duvet tucked under her chin, she lost her balance, pinging the cog from its place and sending wheels and springs spilling out on to the bed. Freya groaned. She supposed that breaking something entirely might be a good way to learn how it worked but it wasn't exactly what she'd been planning. She scrabbled around on the mattress, trying to collect the fallen pieces.

A strange whispering sound reached her and her eyes jerked up towards the vent in the wall. Holding her breath, she tiptoed over and pressed her ear to it. She couldn't imagine what anyone was doing in Edge in February, and it struck her as very odd that Ms Oleander didn't seem to know what she was doing here either. Or if she knew, she certainly wasn't telling. Freya couldn't hear anything. Maybe the sound had just been the wind.

She dragged herself out of bed, pulling on a pair of old jeans and her cosiest, ugliest jumper. She headed to the kitchen to make herself some breakfast. She wondered if Granny Kate would have the fire lit in the breakfast room and headed towards it. At the sound of Ms Oleander's voice Freya paused with one shoulder to the door and a tray in her arms.

"I'm surprised to find such a beautiful place completely empty," came Ms Oleander's voice.

Granny Kate made a non-committal noise

in response.

Ms Oleander pressed on. "I imagine the place is simply bustling with visitors most of the time."

"We're a seasonal business," said Granny Kate. "We do our best trade during the summer months."

"And that doesn't make things difficult for you?"

A tightness crept into Granny Kate's voice. "We get by."

Freya winced. Granny Kate was doing her best to sound breezy, but Freya couldn't help picturing the empty visitor book: Ms Oleander's name standing out stark and black.

Ms Oleander laughed, a strange murmuring sound.

Freya didn't want to listen any more. Instead of the breakfast room, she settled in her bedroom. A steaming mug of tea cooled beside her, accompanied by a slab of Granny Kate's gingerbread loaf, sticky and gleaming with jewels of ginger. Sir Lancelot lounged on the floor beside her, licking gingerbread crumbs from the rug and generally getting in the way.

Her room was the smallest in the B&B but she didn't mind. In fact, she loved it. She loved how it felt like a little burrow. She loved the view of the seagull's nest in the lamp-post opposite. She loved the patchwork rug Granny Kate had sewn to cover the knotty wooden floorboards. Freya had made bunting from the leftover scraps of fabric and it darted cheerfully across the ceiling, painting bright dashes of colour on the white walls, refusing to be dulled by even the dreariest Edge weather.

Much of the room was taken up with Freya's inventing studio, presided over by a much beloved photograph of Nancy Johnson. Nancy Johnson was Freya's hero; she had invented the ice-cream maker.

There were other photos too: of Granny Kate, of Freya and her best friend Lin, of birthdays and picnics and school trips, but Nancy took pride of place. Someday Freya thought she might invent something just as wonderful as an ice-cream maker. Maybe another young inventor would end up with Freya's picture on their wall. But right now she'd settle for managing to put the dismantled reception clock back together. Freya's desk was an old-fashioned writing desk, with a series of drawers and dookits for storing pens and pencils. The clock pieces were spread over its surface.

She turned a spiky cog over between her fingers. She had always been fascinated by how things worked. When she was eight, her Granny Kate had bought her a puzzle box. At first glance it had looked entirely normal: just a rectangular wooden box with a flat lid. But when she tried to pull the lid off, she found that it was stuck. The box was cleverly designed, with a series of hidden panels and switches that had to be arranged in exactly the right way before it would open. It had taken three days for Freya to open it, three days during which Granny Kate had enjoyed glorious, unprecedented silence. She then spent a further three days dismantling it entirely and studying its inner workings before piecing it back together.

Granny Kate's head poked round the door. Freya jumped. Her granny had a talent for materialising out of nowhere, particularly when Freya was doing something she shouldn't be.

"Freya, Lin's at the door for you." She raised

an eyebrow. "I hope that wasn't gingerbread for breakfast."

Freya swallowed. "No," she said, tongue still gummy with treacle.

Granny Kate sniffed. "Make sure you take a piece of fruit on your way out. You'll get scurvy."

Freya swept past her with a kiss and clattered down the stairs. She grabbed her coat and her backpack, begrudgingly shoving an apple in her pocket. She headed out to where her best friend was waiting.

Other than Freya and Lin, the beach was deserted. The rain had stopped but the wind was still howling. Even the most dedicated cold-water swimmers weren't braving the iron sea today. Freya rubbed a sleeve over her glasses in an attempt to clean them but only succeeded in smudging them more. She took them off and cleaned them properly before shoving them back on her face. She ran to catch up with Lin, who was methodically sweeping a metal detector back and forth across the sand.

The metal detector had been Freya's idea. She

was delighted by its clever mechanics, although she hadn't been brave enough to take it apart yet. She had suggested that she and Lin pool their pocket money and buy one. Lin was an avid collector, her bedroom filled with feathers and sea glass and other things she'd found in the surf, so she had immediately agreed. Freya told Lin she was looking for inventing supplies. Secretly she wondered if they might find some treasure. Maybe enough treasure to help Granny Kate with the B&B.

Lin was wearing so many layers of knitwear that she was almost spherical. She was looking back at Freya expectantly.

"Did you say something?" said Freya. "I can't hear you through all your layers."

Lin tugged down the scarf that was covering her mouth. "I said I'm actually freezing."

Freya laughed. "You look actually freezing."

She took the detector from Lin and started to move it in long, sweeping arcs.

Lin shoved her mittened hands into her pockets. There was a little crease between her eyebrows.

"What are you doing your presentation on next week?" she asked.

Every year for citizenship week, each student in the school had to prepare a presentation on one change they'd make to improve Edge. The best from each class was selected and presented in front of the whole school. Lin's sister Mei had been chosen as the best in school last year. And the year before.

The thought of getting up in front of people to talk about anything made Freya want to be sick. In fact, last year she had managed to get out of her presentation by fainting as she stood up to deliver it. She winced and tried to shake the memory from her head.

"Funding for more after-school clubs," said Freya. "I want to start a robotics society but the school says there's no money."

"That's a really good one!"

"Thanks. What about yours?"

"Repairing the ramp from the boardwalk to the beach. The stairs are so awkward for my mum with her stick. Everyone should be able to use the beach."

"They definitely should! That'd be great."

Lin made a face. "Not as good as Mei's."

"What's Mei doing hers on?"

Lin shrugged. "Don't know. But you just know it's going to be better."

"I do not know that. And neither do you."

Lin shrugged again and turned away. Freya could see the hard set of her shoulders even through her puffy coat. She hefted the metal detector into one arm and linked her other arm through Lin's.

Lin squeezed back. "How are you feeling about yours?"

Freya bit her lip. "I'm really nervous."

"Because of last year? No one even remembers that."

Freya rolled her eyes. "One, yes, they definitely do. And two, I fainted because I was nervous; I'm not nervous because I fainted."

"I don't get it," said Lin. "You talk to people all the time at the B&B and you're not scared of them."

Freya chewed her lip. "Not usually, no."

"What does that mean?"

Freya shook her head. "I don't know. This woman checked in yesterday—"

"Into the B&B?" interrupted Lin.

"Obviously," said Freya.

"In February?" said Lin.

"In February! That's weird, right?"

Lin frowned. "I guess. And you're scared of her?"

"Not scared, exactly," said Freya. "I just … I don't know. There was something strange about her."

Lin narrowed her eyes against the drizzle blowing into her face. "Well, yeah. Who comes to Edge in February? I don't want to be here in February and I actually live here."

"Your mum is going to kill you if you don't stop saying 'actually'."

Lin rolled her eyes.

"And if you don't stop rolling your eyes."

"Well, it doesn't sound like anything to be worried about to me. I thought you'd be happy to have someone checking in. I know it can be a bit tough on your Granny Kate in the winter."

"Yeah, you're probably right," said Freya, sounding

extremely unconvinced.

Lin gave Freya's arm another squeeze. "You don't need to be so scared of everything all the time, you know."

Freya disentangled herself from Lin and folded her arms. "I am not scared of everything all the time," she said, even though she was a little bit.

"You are a little bit," said Lin.

"I am *not*."

Lin raised an eyebrow. Well, Freya thought she did. Her woolly hat had twitched.

"So if I was to suggest taking the metal detector over to the caves...?" said Lin.

"Definitely not."

"Why not? If I was a pirate that's where I'd put my treasure."

"We're not going into the caves."

"Because they're haunted?"

"No! Because they're dangerous," said Freya, even though it was a little bit because the caves were haunted.

The cliffs of Edge were riddled with caves, some

burrowing into secret smugglers' passages in town. They ranged from tiny alcoves barely big enough to poke your head in, to huge gaping mouths that echoed with lapping waves and swallowed the light from a torch into nothing. They made sound travel strangely on the beaches, snippets of conversation floating to you even when no one was around – soft moans disappearing into the misty air.

"What do *you* think makes those noises then?" asked Freya.

"I don't know. Not ghosts," said Lin.

It was a source of constant bickering between them. Freya's vivid imagination allowed her to construct and deconstruct complicated puzzles. She could hold a machine in her mind's eye and see how every piece of it fitted together. But that same imagination filled her mind with monsters, just waiting for her to let her guard down. Whereas Lin didn't believe in anything she couldn't see.

She took the detector from Freya and marched ahead, moodily sweeping it in an arc. Her expression immediately cleared as the machine gave a beep.

This was the best thing about Lin. When it came to being cross, she had no attention span at all. In fact, when it came to most things, she had no attention span at all.

She moved the head of the detector in small circles over the sand and, once she was satisfied, she marked a little "x" on the ground with the toe of her boot.

"Treasure!" she shouted. "Spade, please."

Freya dug around in the backpack she was carrying and pulled out a small trowel. She handed it to Lin, who crouched in the sand. "Be careful," Freya said seriously. "If it's treasure, it could be booby-trapped."

"Aye aye, m'hearty. We will proceed with great caution."

She then began whacking at the frozen sand with the blade of the trowel. Freya giggled. Lin started prodding gently into the sand with her fingers, which is easier said than done in mittens.

"Gold!" she yelled. "There's gold in them hills!"

Freya snorted. "I'm pretty sure that's prospectors, not pirates."

"Same thing really."

"Just without boats."

Freya hunkered down beside Lin and the two kept digging with their hands. It wasn't long before Freya's fingers closed round something small and cold. She pulled it from the ground and dusted away the biggest clumps of sand.

"Oh," she said quietly. "It *is* gold."

It was a small coin. Even in the thin grey sunlight, its shine was warm and golden, like melting butter.

Lin pressed in close beside her. "Whoa," she said. "Let me see!"

She took the coin from Freya, holding it close to her face.

"Treasure!" she shouted. "It's treasure!"

Lin's sudden yell made Freya jump, then the two of them dissolved into giggles. They'd found mountains of stuff in the sand since buying the metal detector, filling their pockets with cans and pins and little metal buttons. But they'd never found anything like this before. They burst into a wild impromptu jig, spinning each other on the sand until Lin tripped over the metal detector and fell backwards with a soft *oof*. Freya helped her back to her feet, delighted giggles still bubbling up in her chest.

Lin handed the coin back to Freya and picked up the metal detector. "Maybe there's another couple of million of these under there somewhere," she said.

They swept the metal detector around hopefully, but it stayed stubbornly silent.

Freya slipped the coin into her pocket.

Three

After the cold of the beach, opening the door to Lin's house felt like opening the door of an oven. Freya's fingertips burned as the blood rushed back to them, meaning that it took her three goes to untie her shoelaces. She left her shoes by the front door and followed Lin through to the kitchen. This house was almost as familiar to Freya as her own. She was pretty sure she'd be able to find her way around blindfolded. In fact, she and Lin had tried it once, but Lin's mum put a quick stop to that after Freya had fallen spectacularly down the stairs.

The warm kitchen was the perfect antidote to the beach; the windows steamed, the air gently spiked with ginger and soy. An assortment of Tupperware boxes sat on the counter and Freya sat on her hands to remove the temptation to stick her fingers in them. On the other side of the table Lin's sister Mei and her girlfriend Harpreet sat surrounded by sheets of paper. The two sisters could hardly have looked less alike. Mei was all angles and sharp edges, where Lin was all dimpled softness. They both had waterfalls of shiny blue-black hair, which Freya coveted, and which both sisters saw as a nuisance. But on her fourteenth birthday Mei had hers chopped to her chin and dyed a bright-purple streak in it.

Harpreet looked up and gave Freya a little smile. "Hi, Freya, how are things?"

"Good, thanks. What are you up to?"

Mei rubbed her face, leaving a smudge of ink on her nose. "We're starting a letter-writing campaign. The water pollution around Edge is affecting the algae."

"Oh, the algae," said Lin, sliding into the chair beside Freya and passing her a tiny round bun.

It burned Freya's fingers but it smelled too good to resist. She stuffed it into her mouth, immediately burning her tongue as well.

Mei put down her pen and fixed Lin with a serious look. "It's not funny. The algae are the basis of the whole ecosystem. If the algae are out of whack, it can have really serious consequences."

"Out of Whack Algae would be a great name for a punk band," said Freya.

"Totally," said Lin, just as her mother walked into the kitchen.

Her mum sighed heavily. "Totally, totally. Who speaks like this?"

"Everyone," said Lin.

Lin's mum tapped the back of Lin's chair with her walking stick. "Well, my daughters are not *everyone*." She turned to the counter and started snapping lids on to the Tupperware containers. She froze and turned back towards the girls. "Did someone take one of my buns?"

Lin froze. Freya shoved her burned tongue towards the back of her mouth and adopted what she hoped was an innocent expression.

"I had four more of these," said Lin's mum.

Freya bit back a giggle as she looked across at Mei and Harpreet, who had equally angelic looks plastered across their faces. Lin's mum sighed again, stacked the containers and bustled out of the room, muttering under her breath. Nervous grins broke out round the table.

"So the algae urgently need our help then?" said Lin, drawing another glare from Mei.

Mei always had a cause on the go. She and Harpreet were forever making posters and signing petitions and taking the bus into the nearby city to join protests.

"If you're going to annoy us, you might as well be helpful," said Mei, pushing a stack of papers over towards them. "Write a letter for us. I've got a template here. We're going to present them at the town meeting next week."

"Freya, do you think your granny would write one for us?" asked Harpreet.

"Sure, I could probably get her to care about algae."

"Who wouldn't?" said Lin earnestly, earning a kick from Mei under the table.

"Hey!" she yelled.

"Lin, stop yelling!" yelled her mother from the next room.

"Mei started it!"

"You're still yelling!"

Mei made a smug face at Lin and turned back to her letter.

Freya stuck the template in her bag and glanced at the window. "It's getting dark out there. I'd better be getting back."

Lin looked out of the window and groaned. "It's basically lunchtime. I hate February. Do you want us to walk you back?"

"No, that's all right," said Freya, even though she did. She pushed back her chair and shrugged her coat over her shoulders.

Lin followed her to the door. "You sure you don't want some company?"

Freya shoved her feet into her shoes and shook her head. "Then you'll just have to walk back here on your own."

Lin nodded seriously. "And I might get eaten by a sea monster."

Freya shoved her. "I don't think I'm going to get eaten by a sea monster."

"Kidnapped by a ghost?"

"OK, I'm leaving now."

Lin squished her into a hug. "Let me know when you get home."

Freya squeezed her back and stepped out into the dwindling light. She forced herself to walk slowly while she was in view of the house. But as the bright windows faded behind her she sped up towards the lights of the town. Lin lived just a few minutes away from the town centre but there weren't many street lights along this part of the seafront, so the warmth of the town made the road feel even darker.

The sea whispered beside her, a black expanse stretching out towards the horizon. And off in the distance the wind moaned strangely through the caves. Freya bit down on her lip and started to run. Even as her brain told her she was being silly, her legs propelled her forward. Her glasses slipped down her nose and her skin grew damp under her heavy coat. She reached the town hall, which loomed tall and black in the orange street lights. She leaned against it, trying to catch her breath. She shook her head. Standing in the light, she knew there were no ghosts, no haunted caves, nothing waiting to grab her in the shadows. So why did it feel so hard to believe that in the dark? Lin was right. She had to stop being so afraid of everything. Maybe she'd go and stand back over by the seafront for a few minutes, just to prove to herself that there was nothing there. She chewed her lip and stared at the dark edge of the promenade. The longer she stared, the more the dark seemed to move.

The door to her left banged open and the fright sent her flying instinctively round the corner. She peeked back round the wall. It was, once again, not a monster. It was two people. The hairs on the back of Freya's neck prickled as she recognised Ms Oleander. What was she doing at the town hall? She was packing a sheaf of papers into a document bag.

As she stepped to the side, Freya saw that she was speaking to the mayor of Edge. They shook hands brusquely and a smile crept over Ms Oleander's face as she turned away from him. She buckled her bag, turned up the collar of her coat against the wind and headed in the direction of the B&B.

A flicker of movement pulled Freya's attention away from Ms Oleander. The shadows by the sea seemed to be shifting again. Freya put a hand on the wall to steady herself, her dry mouth clicking as she swallowed. A figure started to take shape in the darkness.

It's not there, thought Freya. *There's nothing there.* Her glasses were blurry with the rain, that was all. She took them off, forcing herself to clean them slowly, trying to push away the thought that something was creeping towards her.

When she put her glasses back on, she had to shove a scream back down her throat. Because there was something there. She could make out a thin, pale face, a glimpse of hair that looked red in the orangey street lights and a pair of dark eyes peering intently towards her. A boy. Freya shuddered as his eyes locked on to hers. The boy was looking at her like he hated her. She stood absolutely still, her eyes pricking in the cold as she struggled to keep the boy in her sight. When she blinked, he was gone.

Four

Citizenship week started with a class trip. Freya's class traipsed out to the old lighthouse, which had been fixed up a few years ago following an extremely successful citizenship week speech by a student. The school's head teacher loved to show it off to her students as an example of what they could achieve by speaking up for the things they cared about. It would probably have been more inspiring if it wasn't February.

They huddled together miserably, soaked by the thin rain and the spray coming off the sea. They climbed endless spiral stairs and stood shivering in the room that used to be the lighthouse keeper's quarters. Freya knew the legend about the pirate who'd washed up here with a diamond, and tried to listen to the tour guide carefully, just in case there were any hints about treasure to be found in Edge's sands, but history had never been Freya's strong suit, and as the guide entered what felt like her fourteenth hour of talking about traditional nautical trades, Freya found her attention waning.

Lin was beside her, similarly distracted and covertly solving a Rubik's Cube. Freya frowned. Puzzles were her speciality but for some reason she had never got the hang of the Rubik's Cube. She suspected this was half the reason that Lin liked them so much. Just to annoy her.

She nudged Lin. "Would you stop that? I'm trying to concentrate."

Lin stuck her tongue out at Freya and carried on.

Freya sighed and tried to zone back in to what the guide was saying. She seemed to be talking about the history of whaling. Freya caught the eye of her teacher, who jerked her head murderously at Lin. Lin obliviously kept at her puzzle. Freya nudged her.

Lin looked up, huffed extravagantly and shoved the Rubik's Cube into her pocket. She slouched against the wall, barely even pretending to listen to the guide. Then she suddenly brightened and darted her eyes towards a painting on the wall.

"Check it out," she said. "I love how mermaids always look sort of evil."

Freya followed Lin's gaze to the painting of the mermaid. She did look a bit evil: long hair swirling around her, dark eyes, small white teeth bared.

"She looks like Ms Oleander," said Freya.

Lin groaned. "You are *obsessed* with this woman."

"I am not *obsessed*. I just think there might be something weird going on."

Lin fixed Freya with a look.

"What?" she said.

"Do you remember the time you thought the school inspector was a spy?"

Heat rushed to Freya's face. "What's that got to do with anything?"

"Or the time you called the police because you thought the window cleaner was trying to burgle the B&B?"

"OK, we said we'd never speak of that again."

Lin bit back a smile. "I'm just saying. You have a habit of going straight for the most exciting explanation. And I'm not sure Edge is as exciting as you think it is. My mum says it's the safest place she's ever lived, and safe is absolutely code for 'most boring'."

The tour guide stopped talking and opened a door on the far side of the room. Freya sighed as yet more stairs came into view.

"Sir Lancelot doesn't like her."

Lin frowned. "My mum?"

"No! Ms Oleander."

Lin gave Freya a gentle shove. "All right, all right. Sir Lancelot doesn't really like anyone, though."

"He likes us."

"That's because we feed him tuna sandwiches. And *that's* why he's the size of a small car."

Freya blew a strand of hair out of her face as they began to climb. She thought of Ms Oleander: her glassy eyes, her gleaming smile. The back of her neck prickled. "She reminded me of an insect or something. Beautiful but in a sort of hard, shiny way."

Lin widened her eyes in mock horror. "Maybe that's it. Maybe she's going to poison you. Or bite your head off and eat you."

Freya snorted. "Just you wait. You are going to feel so bad when she eats me."

The students ascended a sturdy ladder one at a time and found themselves squeezed into the tiny room housing the lighthouse's lamp. Freya leaned against the glass and tried to catch her breath after the climb. Lin had her hands pressed against the glass and was gazing out at the town below. Freya fixed her eyes firmly on the guide. Heights made her feel funny.

"The lighthouse keeper would have made the climb we just made multiple times a day to wind the lamp and keep it turning," said the guide, with a gesture towards the ladder they'd come up.

Freya started paying attention properly. "Wind the lamp? What do you mean?"

The guide grasped the enormous wheel underneath the lamp. "This wheel is connected to a weight in the centre of the lighthouse." She gave the wheel a wrench and Freya heard something big move in the belly of the lighthouse. "The lighthouse keeper would turn the wheel to lift the weight, and the weight turns the lamp as it drops." She let go of the wheel and the lamp turned just a fraction.

Freya reached out to trace the wheel with her fingertips. "That," she said, "is the coolest thing I've ever heard."

Five

The excitement of the trip to the lighthouse faded quickly. Class presentations were looming. Freya had been practising hard. She'd stood in front of her mirror and read her speech what felt like a thousand times. She'd recorded the entire thing on her phone and sent it to Lin, who had sent back a recorded pep talk about how great it was. She really wanted to do it. It was silly to be so afraid of something so simple. Besides, maybe it would make the school think again about the after-school clubs. Maybe she could actually make a difference. She shuffled her notecards, the card becoming bent and flimsy in her damp palms.

But when she thought about getting up in front of the class, her chest tightened. She felt like she could hardly breathe. She dug her fingernails into her palm and took a deep, steadying breath. A blurry spot danced across her vision. She sat down on her bed heavily, a lump rising in her throat. She couldn't do it. There was absolutely no way. She rubbed roughly at her eyes with the back of her hands and made her way through to the kitchen, where Granny Kate was enthusiastically seasoning a pan of sausages.

"Granny Kate, I don't think I can go to school today. I don't feel very well." It wasn't technically a lie.

Granny Kate turned, her spatula tucked under her arm and looked Freya over. "Oh, pet, you look awful."

Freya glanced at the mirror. She did look awful. Pasty and blotched, her eyes were tiny and red.

"I'll ring the school. You get yourself back up to bed." Granny Kate turned and gave her pan a wobble. She pursed her lips. "I guess a sausage sandwich isn't going to do you any good if you're feeling peaky. I'll put these in the fridge and do you some toast."

Freya's stomach growled ferociously at the smell of the frying sausages. "No, I suppose not," she said miserably. "Thanks."

She headed back to her room, changed into some comfy clothes and pulled her bedsheets over her head. She sniffled, her face damp in her blanket cave. She didn't even really know what she was crying about. A weight should have been lifted now that she didn't need to do the presentation. But instead of feeling delighted, she just felt flat and sad. She stayed under the covers as Granny Kate tiptoed into the room. After a few moments, she left again, closing the door gently behind her. Freya peeked out from under her sheets. There was a plate of buttered toast and an enormous mug of tea steaming on her desk.

Freya got out of bed, her duvet still wrapped round her, and trudged over to the desk. Her notecards were neatly arranged on top, ready to be grabbed and put in her schoolbag. She tore one into tiny pieces, hoping that might make her feel better, but it didn't. She balled up the remaining cards and tossed them in the bin. Nibbling despondently on the corner of her toast, she picked up her puzzle box and started arranging it into a new and interesting shape. The puzzling part of her brain lit up, pushing her misery down just a little.

In the afternoon, Granny Kate knocked gently at the door.

"How are you feeling, pet?" she said, crossing the room and perching on the end of Freya's bed.

Freya pulled the blankets up to her nose. If she wanted to go to the town meeting, she'd better start making a miraculous recovery. "A little better, I think."

"Good. I've got some things to do in town. Do you think you'll be OK if I leave you for an hour or so?"

"Yeah, I'll be fine. I'll probably just go back to sleep."

"OK, love. I'll be as quick as I can. Text me if you need anything."

Freya's phone was lying on her desk. She had been pointedly ignoring its buzzing for most of the day.

Granny Kate smoothed a cool hand over Freya's forehead and tiptoed out again. Freya waited until she heard the click of the front door, counted to ten, counted to ten again just to be safe, and then threw off the covers. She was starving.

The air felt freezing after a whole morning under her duvet, so she tugged a fluffy jumper over her head and headed for the kitchen. She made herself a towering cheese and ham sandwich, stuffing the first triangle into her mouth in one bite. She snipped off a bunch of grapes, poured herself a glass of chocolate milk and took three ginger biscuits for good measure. She took her feast through to the breakfast room to enjoy. She loved the little room but she hadn't eaten in there since Ms Oleander had checked in.

It was safe today, though. Freya had heard Ms Oleander leave early this morning. In fact, she hardly seemed to spend any time at the B&B at all, and Freya hadn't seen her in town or on the beaches. The only place she had spotted Ms Oleander so far was outside the town hall. She wondered if that was where the strange woman went when she disappeared, squirrelling herself away to whisper with the mayor.

Sir Lancelot padded into the breakfast room and launched himself on to Freya's lap, knocking the air out of her.

"Oof," said Freya, rearranging him on her knees. "We need to stop feeding you so much. It's not normal for a cat to be this enormous. It's like you're part cat, part stegosaurus."

Sir Lancelot looked up at her and gave a pitiful miaow. Freya sighed and fed him a piece of ham from her sandwich. He leaned against her stomach and settled himself down, vibrating happily.

The door to the B&B rattled open and Freya jumped. She hadn't expected Granny Kate home so soon. She wasn't sure she'd be delighted to see Freya sitting among the remnants of her feast when she was supposed to be too sick to go to school. Her tongue stuck to the roof of her mouth as she heard footsteps clicking towards her. But the door to the breakfast room didn't open. The footsteps passed by and she listened as they faded down the stairs.

Freya frowned. What was Granny Kate doing down in the basement? Freya dithered behind the door for a moment. If her granny stayed down there, Freya would be able to sneak back to her room without being caught.

Very slowly she edged the door to the breakfast room open and peered out into the hall. Granny Kate was nowhere to be seen. Freya started tiptoeing towards her room, wincing as the creaky old floorboards announced her every step. As she reached the edge of the stairs, she peeked over the banister to see if the coast was still clear.

She stopped. It wasn't Granny Kate in the basement. It was Ms Oleander. Her long green coat hung on the end of the banister like a ghost and she had rolled the sleeves of her blouse up to her elbows. Freya watched, hardly breathing, as Ms Oleander padded across the basement, the yellow light of a torch spilling in a circle round her feet. Her lips were moving as though she was counting her steps. Freya heard the woman suck in a sharp breath as her torch picked out the trapdoor in the floor of the basement. Freya didn't know what Ms Oleander could possibly be looking for down there. Her Granny Kate mostly used it to store Christmas decorations and broken bits of furniture. Freya's heart pounded as she watched Ms Oleander reach for the ring on the trapdoor.

Both Freya and Ms Oleander jumped as the door to the B&B rattled open again. Freya leapt back behind the banister as Ms Oleander's head shot up. She dashed across reception, crouching behind the desk. She held her breath as Ms Oleander passed her, sure that the thumping of her heart would give her away. As Ms Oleander's footsteps receded, Freya peeked out over the desk. Lin, standing in the doorway, tugged off her mittens and launched them one at a time at Freya.

"I knew it!" she said. "I brought you some of my mum's magic soup, you big *faker*."

"I'm not faking. I'm actually really sick," croaked Freya.

Lin furrowed her brow. "Come off it, you sound like a Victorian dying of the vapours."

Freya sighed. "We don't have time for this. Come on."

Before Lin had a chance to protest, Freya seized her by the arm and tugged her towards her bedroom. She closed the door quietly behind them, pressed one finger to her lips and darted her eyes meaningfully towards the vent in her wall. The murmuring of a soft voice reached them.

"Is that...?" Lin said.

Freya nodded triumphantly. "I just caught her scrabbling around in our basement. I *told you* she was up to something."

It was hard to make out what Ms Oleander was saying.

"It sounds like she's down a well," said Lin.

Freya nudged her. "If you stop talking, we might be able to hear a little better."

Lin stuck out her tongue but stopped talking, her ear pressed to the wall. Snippets of conversation floated down to the two girls.

"...opportunity to develop ... hidden gem ... real potential..."

"I can't hear anyone else," whispered Freya. "She must be on the phone."

"Amazing deductive skills," said Lin. "You could be a detective."

Freya made a face. She pressed her ear back to the vent. Her brow creased. Something about the way Ms Oleander was talking felt familiar. Something about the cadence of her voice. Freya's eyebrows shot up as she heard Ms Oleander stumble over a word, pause for a second and start her sentence again.

"It's a presentation," hissed Freya. "She's practising a presentation! That's why it's so quiet; she's not actually talking to anyone else."

Lin cupped a hand over her ear and nodded excitedly at Freya. "OK, that actually *was* some pretty good detective work."

They quietened, straining to hear Ms Oleander's faint voice. Now that Freya had realised it was a presentation, the rhythm seemed unmistakable. She caught herself wondering if Ms Oleander felt nervous.

"...and that is why tonight's town meeting is..."

Freya's eyes lit up. She grabbed Lin's hand. "Looks like we're going to the town meeting tonight."

"We were already going to the town meeting tonight," said Lin. "We're going to support Mei with her algae thing."

"That," said Freya, "is not the point."

Six

The town hall was imposing, standing grand and elegant between the main part of town and the ramshackle boardwalk where Freya lived. It was hundreds of years old and looked like an old courthouse. Edge was speckled with these kinds of buildings, harking back to some *before* time that Freya could barely even imagine. The church. The library. The lighthouse. They might have seemed out of place in a more modern town but they were the heart of Edge. Freya always thought Edge seemed like it existed in a time of its own, just a little out of step with the world around it.

The town meeting was busy, with adults jostling for space in the rows of spindly wooden seats. The room was somehow both too hot and too cold, people sweating in their damp winter coats and shivering as the wind crept through the old sandstone walls. Chatter bounced around the enormous room, making it sound odd. It reminded Freya of the sounds that floated out from the caves on the beach. She shuddered and pushed the thought away. She craned her neck, looking for Ms Oleander but there was no sign of her. She couldn't push away the feeling that something big was about to happen. Her leg was bouncing nervously in front of her and she clasped her hands over it to make it stop.

The noise died down as the town council filed in. There were ten of them from all different areas of the town: a teacher, a police officer, a business owner, a handful of parents. They took their seats at the front of the room, seats that Freya noticed looked a whole lot more comfortable than the chairs everyone else was sitting on. They positioned themselves on one side of a long wooden table, shuffling papers importantly and affecting their best serious faces. It made Freya want to giggle and she bit down on the inside of her mouth to suppress the urge. The mayor entered last, his heavy ceremonial chain bouncing on his chest. He pulled in his chair with a scraping sound that set Freya's teeth on edge and called the meeting to order.

At first it was kind of exciting. This was where the big decisions were made. Freya felt delightfully grown-up and nodded along solemnly, regardless of whether she actually understood what had been said. Mei spoke clearly and confidently as she presented the letters she had gathered on the pollution of the beach. Freya swelled with pride as she watched her friend's sister address the council. But after Mei finished, the novelty faded fast. She had managed to pick a wobbly chair and earned herself a death stare from Granny Kate every time the leg clicked against the flagstone floor.

This was worse than assembly. In fact, the longer she listened, the more she thought that her head teacher wouldn't stand for this kind of behaviour in her assemblies. The adults talked over each other. They continued speaking well after their time slot was over. Most of the conversations seemed to descend into the kind of bickering that Freya and her classmates were forever being told off for. And lots of the people speaking didn't really seem to have a question at all, just a long wandering monologue about how everything was better in "the good old days", whenever those were supposed to have happened. Granny Kate tutted gently whenever that one came up and Freya had to bite the inside of her lip. As someone who had started life in a house without an inside toilet, Granny Kate had plenty to say to people who longed for the good old days.

By the time she spotted the familiar flash of green at the front of the hall, Freya had well and truly zoned out. A stab of anxiety pierced her chest. She snapped back to attention.

"It's Ms Oleander," she whispered to Granny Kate.

Granny Kate shushed her gently. Ms Oleander stood

to one side of the council, giving the mayor a small nod.

He cleared his throat. "And now to our last order of business. Ms Vivien Oleander with a proposal for the redevelopment of the Edge seafront."

Freya frowned. What did that mean? A hum of chatter rolled around the room as Ms Oleander walked to the front. She pulled a slim laptop from her bag and looked expectantly at the mayor.

"Oh, right." He pulled on a cord dangling from the ceiling, unrolling a mottled projection screen and dislodging a snowfall of dust and cobwebs on to the rest of the council.

Ms Oleander leapt backwards, a look of distaste curling her features. She brushed off her green coat and plugged her laptop into the whirring projector. A faint image of the seafront flickered into view. The mayor stepped forward and gave the projector a whack. The image sharpened.

Ms Oleander turned her gleaming smile on the waiting audience. "Thank you, everyone, for the warm welcome to your town and for giving me your time and attention this evening. I have an exciting proposal to share with you. One that presents a once-in-a-lifetime opportunity for the town of Edge." Ms Oleander gestured at the photograph behind her. "The Edge boardwalk could be the backbone of this town. It's conveniently located within walking distance of the town centre, with unparalleled sea views."

Freya smiled proudly at the photo. She had always thought the boardwalk was just as wonderful as the sandy beaches on the other side of town. The ancient photobooth. The second-hand bookshop. The penny arcade. The pier with its doughnut stand and rickety helter-skelter. The B&B sat in the middle, painted in soft ice-cream shades of pink and green. Freya could even see her bedroom window in the photo. This was basically like being famous.

"But at the moment it simply isn't living up to its potential." Ms Oleander held up a hand as though someone had started to interrupt her, although no one had. "Yes, it has its charms. Of course it does. But for the most part it is unloved, underdeveloped and choked with dated and dilapidated businesses that are only profitable for a few months of the year."

There was a sharp intake of breath from the audience. Cold anger flushed through Freya. Granny Kate's fingers clamped down on her leg, knuckles white. Her face was chalky, her blusher standing out in scarlet stripes on her face. The town council shifted in their seats, eyes cast towards the floor.

Ms Oleander's smile grew wider still. "This area deserves the attention of someone who can see its potential. Someone who wants it to grow and flourish."

"Someone like you?" came a yell from the back.

Her eyes glittered. "Just so. Someone like me."

She clicked her mouse and the image changed. It took Freya a moment to recognise what she was looking at. It was the seafront again but it was almost unrecognisable. The warped wooden boards had been replaced by a river of smooth tarmac. The soft pastel colours and ramshackle buildings were gone and in their place stood structures that Freya would barely describe as buildings. Slick squares of steel and glass, they looked more like ice cubes. The pier was gone entirely.

"What's that supposed to be?" Freya recognised Mei's voice.

Ms Oleander's smile didn't budge. "The future of the seafront. Luxury residential and retail space."

"And what does that actually mean?" shouted Mei.

"Fancy houses and expensive shops," someone else shouted.

"There are already houses and shops on the boardwalk. Nice ones."

Ms Oleander smoothed down the front of her coat. "It's lovely to see young people so engaged in local politics but I think maybe we should hear from some of the adults in the room. Perhaps the council would like to say a few words about my proposal?"

"It's a fair question from Mei, though," came another voice. Freya peered through the crowd and recognised the patterned hijab of Ms Hanan, her head teacher. "What happens to the people who live and own businesses there already?"

"They will be welcome to rent or purchase space on

the new boardwalk. At the new rates, of course."

Freya almost fell out of her chair as Granny Kate rose to her feet beside her. "I don't know a single person on that boardwalk who'd be able to afford higher rates." Her voice was clear and calm but her hands were shaking.

Ms Oleander gave the mayor a meaningful look.

He cleared his throat and bobbed his head at the audience. "Perhaps we could turn our attention back to Ms Oleander's presentation and save further questions until the end."

Ms Oleander turned back towards the projection screen.

There was a clatter as Mei climbed on to her chair. Harpreet was only a moment behind her.

"Our town is not for sale!" she shouted. "Not for sale! Not for sale!"

Freya watched as Lin clambered on to her seat and took up the chant. She glanced round at the adults, expecting them to follow Mei's lead. Most of them just looked uncomfortable. *Get up*, said Freya internally, half to everyone else in the room, mostly to herself.

This matters, get up. Her mouth felt completely dry. Sweat slicked her palms. Ms Oleander's wide smile looked as though it might crack. Freya licked her lips and started to rise from her seat.

The mayor brought his gavel crashing down loudly on the table. Freya fell back into her seat but Mei, Harpreet and Lin carried on chanting.

"I run a civil meeting here! I will not have all this shouting!" he shouted.

Mei was tugged down from her chair and bustled out of the room, along with Harpreet and Lin. Freya barely heard Granny Kate's protests as she pushed back her chair and ran after them.

Seven

"They can't do this, surely," said Freya, looking at the despondent faces of her friends.

They had taken up residence in the tea room on Edge's main street and were attempting to drown their sorrows in chocolate éclairs. The tea room was a frothing mass of pink and lace and pink lace. The walls were pink. The tablecloths were pink. The cups and saucers were pink. The curtains were patterned gauze, exactly the sort that old ladies have over their windows to peer through. It made Freya feel itchy just to look at. But they did the biggest cakes in town at a price that allowed four kids to turn out their pockets and scrape together enough for a plate of treats. Freya was almost too upset to eat but she did her best, soldiering bravely through one creamy éclair and then another. Mei sombrely poured tea for the group.

Mei shook her head. "It happens all the time in the city. Someone buys up a load of land, builds some glass monstrosity on it and kicks everyone who doesn't like it out."

Harpreet put her hand on Mei's. Mei sighed heavily and started lumping sugar into her tea.

"I guess that explains what she was doing digging around in your basement," said Lin.

Freya frowned. "I guess so," she said, although the more she thought about it, the less sense that seemed to make. "Why would you go looking around a building you planned to knock down?"

Saying it aloud did something funny to Freya's chest and for a moment she thought she might burst into tears. She swallowed hard, poking her fingertips through the lacy cloth on their table.

Lin put her hand on top of Freya's. "We're not going to let that happen," she said.

"It'll go to a vote of the town council," said Harpreet. "They'll decide whether to accept the proposal."

"She's probably got to them already. She wouldn't bring it to the meeting unless she already thought they'd say yes."

Silence descended on the table. Freya stared out the window, watching the sleet break apart on its surface.

"So what do we do?" asked Lin.

Mei shrugged. "I don't know. If she's already got to the council..."

Lin rolled her eyes. "Come on, Mei, isn't this your whole thing? Power to the people and all that?"

Freya nodded. "Lin's right. The town council can't be the only ones who make decisions. And I'll bet we're not the only angry people in Edge right now. So what do we do?"

Mei sucked her teaspoon thoughtfully. "I suppose we could put together a petition and present it to the council."

"Yeah, a petition!" said Freya. "How do we do that?"

Harpreet snorted.

Mei turned to her. "What's so funny?"

Harpreet giggled. "They just grow up so fast, that's all."

Mei laughed.

Lin folded her arms. "We're not *babies*."

Mei waved her hands. "No, we know. It's just nice. Baby activists." She caught sight of Lin's face. "Er, I mean, little activists. Littler than us activists."

"Anyway..." said Harpreet.

"*Anyway*," said Mei, "you're right. The town council might make the final call but they're supposed to be representatives of the town. They can't just do whatever they like. So with a petition you gather signatures in support of a statement you'd like someone in power to consider." She pulled out a notebook. "I can write something and print a bunch of copies. Then we start speaking to people, getting them to add their signature if they agree with us."

Freya's palms started to sweat. "Speaking to people?"

Mei looked up impatiently. "Of course. How else do you think we get people to sign?"

"I don't know. Can we not just post it through all the letter boxes?"

Mei shook her head. "No way. You need to get in front of people and convince them. You want to make it as hard as possible for them to ignore you. If you post it through their door, most people will throw it straight in the bin."

Lin bumped her shoulder against Freya. "Don't worry. We'll do it together."

Freya gave a weak smile and pushed back her chair. She shrugged her shoulders into her coat, a pit settling in her stomach at the thought of having to see Ms Oleander. Lin, seeming to read her thoughts, gave her arm a squeeze as they made their way outside. They dropped arms as Lin struggled to zip up her enormous puffer jacket. She had got a piece of her cardigan trapped in the zip and the angrier she got, the more stuck she became.

Freya turned away so Lin wouldn't see her giggle. The warm light of the tea rooms made the dark evening feel even colder. She blew into her hands and stamped her feet. The cosy bakery across the road looked very far away, a deepening pool of shadow puddling between them. She jumped as a shadow stirred in the alley alongside it. A slender shape crept towards the door and Freya felt goosebumps rush across her skin. It was a boy. He was pale with carroty-red hair, wearing a coat that looked pretty much useless in this kind of weather. Even at a distance it looked like he hadn't washed his face in a long time. Freya frowned. She was quite sure he didn't go to their school, but she felt as though she knew him, as though she'd seen him somewhere before. A woman came bustling out of the bakery, jostling her paper bags as she wrestled with a giant umbrella. The boy darted towards the woman, barging roughly into her. She exclaimed as she lost her balance and gripped the umbrella, dropping her two paper bags. In one fluid movement the boy scooped up the bags, turned and ran.

"Hey!" shouted Freya.

He turned instinctively at her shout and as his dark

eyes met hers, she suddenly realised where she had seen him before. It was the boy who had been staring at her the night she had seen Ms Oleander at the town hall. She was sure of it.

The boy recovered faster than Freya, disappearing back into the alley.

Freya took off after him.

"What the—" yelled Lin, shuffling after Freya. "What are you running for?"

Freya burst out on to the seafront, arms windmilling to stop herself falling headlong into the sand. The beach was almost completely in darkness. The boy was nowhere to be seen. Freya strained her ears, listening for footsteps, but the only thing she could hear was the mournful singing of the caves. That was quickly drowned out as Lin caught up with her, breath puffing out of her in spiralling clouds.

"Well, thank you very much for that unscheduled exercise," she said. "I'm not sure we're dressed for it, though."

"Did you see that boy?" asked Freya.

"A boy?" Lin put her head in her hands. "You know

when they talk about chasing boys, they don't usually mean it literally."

Freya shoved her. "I wasn't chasing him. Well, I was. But not like *that*; don't be so gross. He stole two bags of pastries from a lady outside the bakery."

"Oh, congratulations," said Lin. "I didn't realise you'd been appointed chief of police."

"I wasn't planning to arrest him."

"Well, that's good news."

Freya clamped a hand over Lin's mouth, both of them starting to get the giggles.

"I think I saw him before. What if he's following me?"

Lin's mouth twitched. "Maybe he's terribly in love with you."

"Lin, I'm serious. I thought I'd imagined him the first time but I properly saw him this time."

Lin looked along the empty beach. "Well, there's no one here now. Are you sure that...?"

Freya planted her hands on her hips. "Sure that what?"

Lin raised her palms. "You know you can let your

71

imagination run away with you sometimes."

"I did not *imagine* a boy stealing a pastry."

"I thought it was two bags of pastries."

"It was two bags of pastries."

"This story is shifting by the minute."

Freya seriously considered shoving Lin into the sea. She stuffed her hands in her pockets to stave off the temptation. The wind whistled along the coast, whipping sand into their faces.

Lin rubbed at her eyes. "If you're not planning on performing a citizen's arrest, can we please go home before we die of exposure?"

Eight

Granny Kate's face was sombre at breakfast. Freya pushed a single spoonful of cereal around her bowl until it disintegrated.

"Don't worry, pet," said Granny Kate. "We're going to be all right."

Freya looked up at her, her chin propped in one hand. "You mean we might be able to stay?"

Granny Kate winced. "No, sweetheart. If the proposal goes through, we'd need to find somewhere else to go."

"Like in town?"

Granny Kate was quiet for what felt like a very long time. "Maybe somewhere outside Edge."

Freya started, almost knocking her bowl off the table with her elbow. "You'd think about leaving Edge?"

"We might not have another choice." Granny Kate plastered on a brave smile. "But maybe it'd be exciting. A new adventure."

"I don't want a new adventure! I like this one. What about my school? And my friends?"

"I know it's hard, Freya," said Granny Kate. "I don't really want to go either. But there are schools everywhere. You'd make new friends no problem."

"I like my friends now," yelled Freya. She knew she was being unfair, that it wasn't Granny Kate's fault, but she was too upset to care. "Our whole life is here. It's where you grew up. It's where Mum and Dad grew up."

A heavy silence fell between them, eventually broken by the creak of the stairs above them.

"She'll be down in a minute," said Granny Kate quietly. "If I were you, I'd make yourself scarce."

Granny Kate walked out of the breakfast room, leaving Freya fizzing. She should make herself scarce. She didn't especially want to talk to Ms Oleander. Besides, as part of citizenship week, they had the day off school to volunteer in the community. Freya, Lin, Mei and Harpreet were using theirs to start gathering signatures for their petition. She didn't want to tip Ms Oleander off. She moved towards the door but stopped at the sound of her granny's voice. She held her breath and pressed one eye to the crack in the door.

"I hope you understand it's nothing personal," Ms Oleander was saying. "The B&B is lovely. It's just—"

"Dated and dilapidated," finished Granny Kate.

Ms Oleander at least had the grace to look embarrassed. "Sales pitches. Everything has to be overexaggerated. I'd very much like for you to consider staying on and opening premises in the new development."

"I have neither the cash nor the inclination for that," said Granny Kate. "The old boardwalk has character. That's where my B&B fits."

"Well, I suppose all good things must come to an end," said Ms Oleander, fixing Granny Kate with a dazzling smile.

Granny Kate bounced an equally bright smile back at her. "I suppose they must. But it's not over yet."

Ms Oleander's eyes flashed dark. She put Freya more in mind of an insect than ever. Something colourful and poisonous. Freya clenched her teeth. Her scalp tightened with anger. She grabbed a teacup from one of the unused tables and poured the entire contents of Ms Oleander's sugar bowl into it. She hid it in a corner behind a menu. Then, returning to Ms Oleander's table, she filled the sugar bowl with salt. After a quick glance around to make sure nothing looked amiss, Freya slid the window open, slipped out and headed towards town with her head held high.

Mei had been busy. She had drawn up a list of businesses and a route for them to follow. She had typed and printed their petition, as well as a short script for them to read from. Even so Freya could hardly bring herself to speak to anyone. She dithered at the back of the group, nodding enthusiastically as

Mei and Harpreet took the lead.

In one shop a lady had asked what the people living on the boardwalk thought of the proposals and Freya had unexpectedly found herself thrust into the spotlight. She flushed bright red, stammering through her answer, barely able to remember what she'd said. But the woman had signed the petition, and Freya felt a warm spring of pride open up inside her.

By the time lunchtime rolled around, Freya was ravenous. Mei steered them towards the tea rooms, waving to a young woman sitting at one of the tables by the window.

"Who's that?" whispered Freya.

"No idea," whispered Lin. "I don't recognise her."

The woman stood up as they approached and held out a hand to Mei. She had a mass of curly hair chopped into a bob and her fingertips were smudged with blue ink.

"You must be Mei," she said with a smile.

"I am," said Mei. "And this is everyone."

"Hi, everyone," said the woman. "I'm Lily. I'm a

reporter with the *Edge Chronicle*. I'm here to interview you about your campaign to save the boardwalk."

An interview? Nerves slithered in Freya's belly. No one had said anything about this to her. Although from the look on Lin's face, she hadn't known either. Another woman approached, a camera slung round her neck and three plates of toasties balanced in her hands.

"And this is Sam, my photographer."

Sam put the plates down on the table. Mei took a toastie and did a double take.

"Hang on, I know you! You're Sam! You're the one—"

"The thing with the diamond?" interrupted Sam. "That was me. Well, more Lily, really."

"No!" said Mei. "Well, yes, obviously. But that's not what I was going to say. You started the campaign for gender-neutral bathrooms in the school!"

"Oh!" Sam looked thrilled. "Yes, that one actually was me."

Mei beamed. "Well, my friend Jaz is very grateful. Their school day is a whole lot less stressful thanks to you."

Sam wriggled a little. "I am so, so delighted to hear that."

Lily smiled. She pulled a spiral-bound notebook from her bag. "So, do you want to tell me how you first got interested in saving the boardwalk?"

There was a shy silence. Lily tucked her pencil behind her ear. "I promise there's nothing to be nervous about. We just want to ask you a few questions."

Sam snorted. "I promise she intended that to sound less like what the police say before they arrest you for murdering someone."

Freya felt like her mouth was full of cotton wool. "I think I'll go and have a look at the cakes," she said quietly, slipping out from behind the table and heading for the display case by the cash register.

"Oh, hello, Freya," said Aileen, the lady who owned the tea rooms. "Are you waiting for your granny? You can go through to her if you want."

"Go through to her?"

"Everyone's in the back room," said Aileen, nodding towards the door on the far side of the cafe.

Freya glanced back at her table. Mei was holding

court, the reporter scribbling fast. She didn't think they'd miss her too much. She headed for the back room. A wave of heat hit her as she pushed open the door. There were twelve people in the room, sitting round a large table. Freya recognised her head teacher, Ms Hanan, as well as Lin's mother and a couple of her neighbours from the boardwalk. The chatter in the room fell silent. Freya flushed bright red as twelve sets of eyes swivelled towards her.

"Freya," said Granny Kate, standing up from her chair at the head of the table, "what are you doing here?"

"What am I doing here?" said Freya. "I was eating a toastie. What are you doing here?"

The door opened behind her, and Lin entered, followed by a man with friendly creases around kind brown eyes. Lin gestured at him. "I wondered where you'd gone," she said, "and then I found Harpreet's grandpa hanging around outside. What's going on?" She blinked as she took in the table. "Ma? What are you doing here?"

Harpreet's grandpa stepped smoothly in front of

Freya and Lin.

"I'm Amar Bajwa. Am I in the right place for the campaign to stop the sale of the boardwalk?"

"The what?" chorused Freya and Lin.

Granny Kate bristled with indignation. "Well, really, you didn't imagine I was going to let this woman turf me and my neighbours out of our homes without a fight, did you?" She held out her hand to Mr Bajwa. "Kate Lawson."

Mr Bajwa took Granny Kate's hand in both of his. "It's a pleasure, Ms Lawson."

"Kate's fine."

"Kate, then."

Granny Kate turned pink. Freya and Lin exchanged a look. Granny Kate cleared her throat gently and made her way back to her seat, busying herself with shuffling papers as Mr Bajwa sat down. She gestured to Freya and Lin. "Come on, the two of you might as well sit since you're here."

Freya slid into one of the empty seats.

"I have some good news," said Granny Kate. "The town council has agreed to meet with us."

A quiet murmur rippled round the table.

"The bad news," Granny Kate continued, "is that they would like to meet with us this Saturday. So we have two days."

"We'll be ready for them," said Lin's mother, tapping her stick on the ground for emphasis.

Granny Kate gave a curt nod. "We will." She turned to Freya and Lin. "It's good that both of you are here. I wanted to ask if you, Mei and Harpreet would come with us and present the signatures you've gathered."

Freya's throat creaked as all the moisture drained out of her mouth.

"We'd love to!" squealed Lin, grabbing Freya's hand.

Freya felt dizzy.

Granny Kate gave her a quick wink. "Not to worry, pet – we'll show them what Lawson women are made of. All right, everyone, two days. Let's save the boardwalk. Let's save our home."

Nine

The two days passed in a flurry. They continued to gather signatures for their petition. Granny Kate worked on her presentation. Freya could hear her in the evenings, pacing up and down, murmuring her practised sentences under her breath. And to her horror they had asked Freya to speak about living on the boardwalk.

Freya felt so ill as she got ready to go to the town hall that she had to sit down in the shower, resting her head against the tiles as the water swirled round her. Afterwards she had nibbled half-heartedly at a slice of buttered toast but couldn't stomach more than a few bites. Then the phone shrilled from reception, making her choke, spraying crumbs everywhere. Coughing, she made her way to the desk.

"Bright and Breezy, how can I help you?" she croaked.

She was answered with a snort. "I love your serious telephone voice," said Lin. "I should ring reception more often."

Freya frowned. "Why are you ringing reception?"

"Well, I tried your phone first but you didn't answer."

Freya patted her pocket. No phone. It must be up in her room somewhere.

"I just wanted to see how you were feeling," said Lin.

"You mean whether I was planning to chicken out again?"

"No!" said Lin. "That's not what I mean at all. I knew you'd be nervous and thought you might like to hear a reassuring voice."

"Should have got someone else to call then."

Lin chuckled. "That's the spirit. Did you see the

article in the *Chronicle*?"

"Granny Kate is out picking up a copy now."

Lin laughed. "My mum has bought about nine copies; she's sending them to all my aunties."

"She'll probably wallpaper the front room with them," said Freya.

"Don't even joke. She absolutely would do that."

A small tut echoed down the phone line. There was a pause. Freya held the phone away from her ear as Lin yelled.

"Ma! Stop listening in on my conversations! This is why no one uses the landline any more."

There was a huff and a click.

Lin sighed. "This isn't a secure line. Go and get ready and I'll see you soon. You can do this."

"See you soon," whispered Freya.

Her feet felt heavy as she headed back up the stairs. She dug out a neat checked dress that had hung in her wardrobe since she was given it for Christmas two years ago. It was a little snug under her arms but it was probably the most respectable thing she owned. The fact that she'd never worn it at least meant that there was no chance of it being torn, covered with glue or singed from the very brief period before Granny Kate had confiscated her soldering iron. She wriggled her way into a pair of scratchy tights and put on her school shoes. The toes were a bit scuffed. She sat down on her bed and carefully coloured in the scuffed areas with a black felt-tip pen. She examined her handiwork. You could hardly see the marks now, not unless you were looking for them, and she thought it unlikely that the council would be. She brushed her hair into a high ponytail and looped a ribbon round it for good measure.

She looked at herself in the mirror and gulped heavily. She somehow looked both pasty and blotchy, her eyes shining in her face. She rubbed them defiantly and took a deep, steadying breath. She stepped out of her bedroom, closing the door behind her with a click. This was already further than she'd managed to get with her school presentation. She used this thought to propel herself down the stairs to where Granny Kate was waiting.

* * *

The room they were shown into on arrival at the town hall was small and painted in inoffensive but uninspiring shades of green and grey. Much of it was taken up with an enormous round table. Freya noticed that the seams on several of the chairs were wearing thin, showing tufts of foamy yellow stuffing. The council sat round one side of the table, smiling placidly at them. The mayor sat in the middle, the heavy ceremonial chain round his neck. He shook hands with Granny Kate, fixing her with a smile. Freya didn't like how it clicked into place. It looked like a smile that he carefully put on each morning along with his tie.

Freya fidgeted in her chair as her Granny Kate spoke and then Mei. She tried to focus on what they were saying but all she could think about was the fact that in a minute they'd be asking her to speak. She felt the clammy press of tears against the back of her throat and swallowed hard. The tight seams of her dress cut into her underarms and her back, making it difficult to breathe.

"Freya?"

Freya looked up, scanning the faces of the council for who had spoken. One of the women was smiling gently at her. She had blonde hair set in a bob so smooth and shiny that Freya wondered if it would move if you touched it.

"Hi, Freya. My name is Catherine."

Freya didn't know what she was supposed to say in response.

Catherine continued. "Would I be right in thinking that you're a little nervous about speaking to us today?"

Freya nodded.

"Public speaking can be really hard, I know, but this is just a conversation. There's no wrong thing to say."

Freya tugged at a scrap of skin on her lip. Her eyes darted to the rest of the council.

Catherine shook her head. "Don't worry about them. We're just talking. Just say it to me. Your granny has run the B&B for a long time, is that correct?"

Freya nodded again. "Oh, ages. There's a lady who comes every summer with her family who came to the B&B for her honeymoon. I think that was about forty years ago. She's pretty old."

Catherine laughed. "A bit like myself. We've heard what your granny has to say about the proposal for the new boardwalk, but I'd like to hear what you think. Maybe us old folks are just too set in our ways to see the potential in an idea like Ms Oleander's."

Freya frowned. "No, I don't think so. Just because something's old doesn't mean it's not good."

Catherine laughed again.

Freya drummed her fingertips against the table. She didn't feel like she was explaining herself very well.

"It's just that Edge is weird," she said. "It's not like other places, not even like other seaside towns. That lady who comes to stay with us every summer, she says it's like a place fallen out of time. And that is sort of what it feels like. That's why I like living here. Because it feels like something strange could happen at any moment. That's why I think the boardwalk is worth saving." She clicked the heels of her shoes nervously together. There was a creak from behind her and her chest constricted in anger as she saw Ms

Oleander come through the door. She pulled a chair up to the table and fixed her gleaming eyes on Freya.

Freya swallowed. "If our boardwalk becomes just the same as everywhere else, why would anyone come and visit? Besides, it's not all about the visitors. The boardwalk isn't 'an opportunity' or an 'exciting venture'. It's my home."

Freya glanced over at her Granny Kate. Her eyes looked a little misty. Or maybe Freya's glasses had steamed up. Granny Kate never cried.

The council members murmured to each other, exchanging sheets of notes. The mayor cleared his throat and gestured with an open palm to Ms Oleander.

"Ms Oleander, do you have a statement you would like to make in response?"

Ms Oleander fixed the group with a smile that was as sweet as candyfloss and just as fake.

"Change can be frightening," she said. "I completely understand and sympathise with Freya's feelings. But the fact is that my proposal would be good for this town. Without some serious investment Edge is on a downhill spiral. The businesses are unprofitable. The buildings are falling apart. The services are stretched. If I'm permitted to buy the boardwalk and develop it, just think what the town could do with that money. I'm very sorry that the Lawsons and their friends are unhappy with my proposal, but to refuse my bid would be to put the happiness of a few people before the future of your whole town. And I think, Mr Mayor, that you know better than that."

The mayor steepled his fingers beneath his chin. "We thank you all very much for your contributions today. Council will now retire to our chambers to discuss. You are welcome to wait here for our decision."

The council filed out slowly, Catherine shooting Freya a warm smile before closing the door.

Ten

The silence that filled the room once the council had left seemed enormous. Freya felt like she was drowning in it. She looked round at the faces of her family and friends. They looked tight, drawn, nervous. Ms Oleander was perfectly composed, leaning back in her chair, her hands resting on the table in front of her. She looked like someone who knew she was going to win.

Freya pushed back her chair with a squeal. Everyone jumped.

"I need some fresh air," she said, darting out of the

room before anyone could reply.

She pattered down the steps, across the lobby of the town hall and burst out into the cold February sunshine. She gulped in the freezing sea air gratefully. She crossed the road to the metal rail separating the walkway from the beach below. Her gaze was drawn along to the pretty pastel shutters of the B&B visible in the distance. There was a young woman struggling to manoeuvre a buggy over the uneven planks of the boardwalk. Her baby gave a yelp as one wheel wedged itself behind a sunken plank, jostling the buggy.

Freya felt the familiar shape of Lin squeeze in beside her.

"You OK?" asked Lin.

"Not really," said Freya. "You?"

"No, not really." Lin nudged Freya. "You were so great in there. I can't believe how well you did."

Freya laughed. "I felt like I was going to be sick."

"Well done for not doing that."

Freya squeezed the rail in front of her. A flake of rust loosened and wedged itself in her palm. "I was just thinking about something Ms Oleander said."

Lin raised her eyebrows. "Well, that seems like a mistake."

"This place *is* falling apart. Maybe it does need a bit of a makeover."

Lin jerked backwards. "You can't mean you think the sale should go through?"

Freya gave Lin a shove. "No! Of course not. I just mean the town really does need some money to fix things up."

Lin nodded her head back towards the town hall. Granny Kate was standing in the window waving to them. "I guess we'll find out now," said Lin.

Freya's stomach felt like it was full of snakes as they climbed the steps back up to the room. Freya sank back into her seat, prodding at a tuft of spongey yellow stuffing with one finger. Mei sat poker straight beside her, her hand laced through Harpreet's. Both their knuckles were white. The mayor cleared his throat gently and Freya snapped back to attention.

"We were incredibly impressed with the quality of your presentation this morning. You have gathered some fantastic insights from the community and presented them to us in a clear and interesting way."

Freya's heart gave a flutter. That sounded good. It sounded really good. She glanced over at Catherine, the friendly lady with the blonde bob, and gave her a little smile. Catherine cut her eyes away and Freya felt something plummet fast and hard through her centre. She barely registered the cymbal crash of the mayor's "but". That look had been enough. She understood immediately and devastatingly that they had lost.

"But," the mayor said, "we have been unable to decide in your favour today. The proposal made by Ms Oleander is simply too compelling and holds too much benefit for the town as a whole."

A murmur of outrage rippled through the room.

"What benefits does it bring?" said Harpreet.

"Money," said Granny Kate. "He's talking about money."

Mei's head jerked up. "That can't be the only thing that matters. What about the town?"

The mayor fixed them with a patronising look. "This is for the good of the town."

"How can ripping its heart out be good for the town?" said Mei.

Fuzzy spots danced in front of Freya's vision. She turned to look at Granny Kate. She was entirely grey, a hand resting limply over her mouth. Lin's mum was exactly the opposite. She looked as though she had been boiled, her face almost purple with rage.

"I understand this is likely to come as a disappointment to you," the mayor said.

"I don't think you do," said Harpreet. "I don't think you understand at all."

The mayor acted as though he hadn't heard her. "Unfortunately the council's decision on this matter is final. I hope this won't discourage you from bringing further issues to the council in future. We are here to listen and to represent your concerns."

"Until someone with bigger pockets than us comes along," said Mei.

The mayor's face twisted, as if he was smelling something unpleasant. "I'm sorry that we weren't able to give you the response you were looking for. But I assure you that we very much appreciate your efforts and that we considered your case very carefully before coming to our decision." He rapped the table. "The sale of the town boardwalk will move ahead. All current businesses and residents will receive details of the new arrangements in writing. Contracts are expected to complete in two weeks."

Eleven

Freya was at Lin's front door by eight o'clock the next morning. She barely had time to knock before Lin pulled the door open.

"Couldn't sleep?" asked Lin.

Freya shook her head.

"Me neither," said Lin. "Come on in."

Freya followed Lin through to the kitchen.

"Whoa," she said.

The counters were crowded with pots and containers.

"Ma has been stress-cooking," said Lin, gesturing at

the chaos around them.

"Well, at least some good came out of all this," said Freya.

Lin smiled weakly at the joke.

A pot caught Freya's eye. "Is that magic soup?"

Lin smiled. "What else?"

"And what's the policy on soup for breakfast?"

"Soup is always a good idea."

Lin ladled out two bowls of her mum's magic soup, a shimmering golden broth that promised to heal anything that ailed you. Got the flu? Magic soup. Stubbed your toe? Magic soup. Fell out with a friend? Magic soup. Freya lifted the bowl to her lips and took a long sip. It didn't fix the fact that she was about to lose her home, but it definitely made her feel better. She set her bowl down. "This can't just be it," she said.

"I was thinking exactly the same," said Lin. "There's always a way out."

Freya drummed her fingertips on the ceramic bowl.

"Come on," said Lin. "Out with it."

Freya frowned. "Out with what?"

"Whatever it is that you were just thinking about

saying but decided not to."

Freya's mouth twitched. It was a nightmare being friends with someone who knew you so well.

"I was just thinking..." she said, her cheeks flushing.

Lin clicked her fingers. "Less thinking, more speaking."

Freya sighed. "What about the metal detector?"

"The metal detector?"

Freya's blush deepened. "Do you remember the coin we found?"

"Of course," said Lin, "and it's lovely, but I doubt the council are going to let us buy the boardwalk with it."

"What if there were more?"

Lin pursed her lips. She didn't look convinced.

"Or do you just want to come over and help me pack?" said Freya crossly.

Lin held up a hand. "Of course not. Just give me a minute."

Freya took another sip of her soup.

Lin sighed. "I don't know, Freya. We've been over that beach a million times and, other than that one coin, all we've turned up is a load of junk."

Freya nibbled at the skin round her thumbnail. She had already thought of that. In fact, she'd been thinking about it since yesterday.

"Maybe," she said, "if you want to find something you've never found, you have to look somewhere you've never looked."

Lin's brow creased, and then her face lit up with a wicked little grin. "Are you serious? You're up for going into the caves?"

Freya immediately regretted having said it. But she couldn't just stand by and let Ms Oleander win. She shrugged. "It's like you said before: if I was a pirate that's where I'd put my treasure."

"Oh," said Lin, "this is going to be fun. Finish that soup and let's go."

The last remnants of Freya's courage deserted her as they approached the yawning mouth of the first cave. Lin, leading the way, held the torch. Freya had the metal detector. Lin marched forward confidently, while Freya dithered at the entrance.

The temperature dropped as she stepped inside. She shuddered and ran to catch up with the thin beam of Lin's torch. The wind moved through the caves, strange moaning sounds rising around them.

"This is awesome," said Lin, swinging her torch around the space.

Freya didn't reply. It didn't feel awesome to her at all. Lin's torch drew away from her again. "Lin, wait!" she called. "Slow down!"

Lin turned back, pointing her torch at Freya. "If there's something here, it's not going to be at the very front, is it? We have to go in."

"We are in."

Lin planted her hands on her hips. "We're about two steps in. Come on. I thought you wanted to do this properly."

"Just don't go so fast," said Freya. "I don't want to get lost."

"You're not going to get lost – don't be such a baby."

"It's not being a baby to be careful when you're doing something dangerous."

"It *is* being a baby to be more scared of the dark

than of losing your home."

Freya's nose filled with the fizz of tears. "I'm not scared of the dark."

"Good," said Lin. "Then let's go."

As the light from the cave mouth receded behind them, Freya swept the metal detector in tight arcs, hunching her shoulders against the cold. The detector's gentle beep bounced off the craggy walls, turning strange and alien. She tried not to think about rockslides or caves flooding. She tried not to think about stories in which children wandered off the path and were lost in the dark forever.

She realised that she could hardly see where she was going. Lin was far ahead of her, and the beam of the torch looked tiny and impossibly far away. She rushed to catch up, taking a vicious gouge out of her ankle with the metal detector.

"Lin," she called. "Lin, wait for me."

She hated the way her voice sounded, thin and shaky and terrified.

"It's OK," shouted Lin. "I just thought I saw—"

Her voice cut off with an odd muffled sound and

the torchlight disappeared completely. Ice settled in Freya's insides. She couldn't see anything. She opened her eyes wide, willing them to adjust to the dark, but she couldn't even make out how far away the walls were.

"Lin?" she called again. "Lin, where are you?"

There was no response.

"Lin, this isn't funny."

A skittering sound arose to one side of her and she wheeled round. Her heart felt like it might burst, her blood drumming in her chest and throat and fingertips. She couldn't remember which way she had been facing. She couldn't remember which way was out. Her eyes pricked and she swallowed hard.

Don't panic, she told herself. *Don't panic*.

"Lin," she croaked, her breath whistling in and out of her chest.

There was a tiny shifting sound behind her and cold fingers slipped round her neck. She screamed, dropping the metal detector and bolting. She didn't know which direction she was running; she just knew that she had to get away from whatever was in the cave with her. A second sound mingled with her echoing scream and it took her a moment to place it. Someone was laughing.

Lin clicked the torch back on and shone it up into her face. She was leaning against the cave wall, doubled over with laughter.

"I'm sorry, I'm sorry, but that was so funny. You are *definitely* scared of the dark."

Freya couldn't even speak. Her mouth tasted bitter and coppery and she realised that she'd bitten her tongue.

Lin swept the torch around until she found the dropped metal detector. "Oh man," she said, dusting it off. "I hope this isn't broken. Honestly, you should have seen your face."

Freya burst into huge shuddering sobs.

Lin's mouth dropped open and she rushed over to Freya.

"Hey, it's all right; it was just a joke. You don't need to get upset." She put an arm round Freya.

"Don't touch me!" Freya shoved her away a little more roughly than she had meant to.

Lin stumbled backwards, sitting down hard in a pool of cold water. She cried out as the water seeped through her jeans. She lifted up a hand and looked at it with wide eyes. It was speckled with tiny scratches, a few welling red.

"What is *wrong* with you?" she shouted.

"What's wrong with me? What's wrong with *you*?" Freya shouted back.

"Oh, come on," said Lin. "I'm trying to show you that there's nothing to be scared of. It's always just your imagination."

Freya snatched the torch from Lin and headed back towards the beach.

Lin followed behind, dragging the metal detector. "Wait!" she called. "You're seriously that angry?"

Freya didn't answer; she just kept ploughing forward towards the rocky beach.

"Freya! Come on, I didn't mean to scare you."

Freya spun round and Lin almost walked into her.

"Are you kidding me? You didn't mean it? What, were you hexed by a wizard? Possessed by a haunted doll? You just tripped and needed to use my neck to steady yourself?"

"No!" yelled Lin. "Obviously not!"

Freya threw up her hands. "What are you yelling at me for?"

"I'm not!" yelled Lin. She rubbed a hand across her forehead. "I just thought you were freaking yourself out, so if you got the fright out of the way, you'd realise you were being silly. I really thought you'd laugh."

"If you paid attention to a single thing I say, ever, you'd know I wouldn't laugh."

"That is so not fair. All we ever do is talk about you. Your granny. Your B&B. Your thing with Ms Oleander."

Freya winced as though Lin had hit her. She felt the tightness of tears again. "Well, if that's how you feel, maybe we shouldn't be friends any more."

Lin flushed bright red, her eyes shining. "Fine, maybe we shouldn't."

She tucked the metal detector under her arm, spun on her heel and stormed away, leaving Freya standing alone in the dark mouth of the cave.

Twelve

A lump sat heavy in Freya's chest as she got ready for school on Monday morning. It had been the worst weekend she could remember. She dawdled in the corridor until the last minute, only entering the classroom when she couldn't put it off any longer. Lin was sitting in her usual seat and her eyes widened hopefully as Freya walked in.

Freya sat down and started to silently unpack her bag.

"Freya," hissed Lin.

Freya kept her eyes fixed downwards.

"Hey," whispered Lin, "please can we talk about this?"

Freya fumed. This was so typically Lin, just expecting everything to be fine. She leaned her chin in one hand, blocking Lin with her arm.

"You're seriously not going to talk to me?"

Freya put up her hand. "Miss, Lin won't stop talking to me. Can I move seats?"

Freya heard Lin's sharp intake of breath but didn't look round.

Their teacher frowned slightly but gestured to an empty seat at the other side of the classroom. "Hurry up then."

Freya felt Lin's eyes on her as she moved. She was focusing so hard on not looking back at Lin that she hardly heard a word of the class. As soon as the bell rang, she darted out of the room, finding a spot at the far edge of the playground where Lin probably wouldn't think to look for her. By the end of the day she was quite sure she'd never felt so lonely in her whole life.

She didn't want to go back to the B&B and face

a deflated Granny Kate or, worse, a triumphant Ms Oleander. And she couldn't go back to Lin's. So she went to the beach, relishing the way the dreary scene echoed her misery. The sea was grey and malignant in the dull light. It was misty, as though the clouds had fallen all the way down and couldn't be bothered hoisting themselves back up again. Tiny snowflakes peppered the sand, staying for a moment before being sucked into the slushy grey sea. Freya shivered. Granny Kate always said the colder it was, the smaller the snowflakes. These were like powder.

Freya frowned, cocking her head. A familiar moaning sound reached across the beach towards her. She dragged her eyes towards the rocks and the dark caves at their edge. The chill of the wind drilled right through her middle and she shivered, turning the collar of her coat up. She grimaced as the action dislodged a few frozen droplets of water and sent them helter-skelter down the back of her neck.

She edged towards the caves in tiny sideways steps like a crab. The wind dropped as she reached the shelter of the cliffs, the fog parting so they stretched out in front of her in all their glory. The strange moaning sounds continued, as though the caves were singing to themselves. She shuddered as she recalled stories she had read. Mermaids singing to lure sailors on to the rocks. Will-o'-the-wisps singing to trick unwary travellers off the path. She drew a squiggle in the wet sand with the toe of her boot.

She cocked her head, listening. The moaning sound seemed to be coming from a tall narrow cave. Temper flared in her chest as she remembered Lin's jab about her being more scared of the caves than she was of losing her home. It wasn't true. She could be brave. She'd prove it. And if she got lost and was never seen again, at least Lin would feel really, really bad.

Freya clicked on her torch and edged forward. She had to squeeze herself into the space sideways, stepping up over a small ridge. Once she was through, the narrow passage branched off to the left. She turned, her puffy coat scraping the rough walls, and continued. The faint light of the beach faded behind her as she rounded the corner. Freya was annoyed at how much her hands were shaking, sending the torch beam darting wildly around.

I can't breathe, she thought, as the walls of the cave pressed in on either side of her.

She planted her palms flat on the wall behind her and rested the back of her head against it. She closed her eyes. She *could* breathe. The space was narrow, but it wasn't that narrow. She was panicking, that was all. She pictured Lin's stubborn face and that was enough to send her barrelling onwards, further into the tunnel. To her enormous relief the space widened out, spitting her into a huge cavern.

The ground here was mostly flat and, thanks to the ridge at the mouth of the cave, surprisingly dry. It was cold, though, and everything glittered with frost. The beam of her torch picked out enormous stalactites dangling from the ceiling like bats, jewelled with barnacles and seashells. The layers of rock that made up the cliffs were more visible here, striping wild marbled patterns all around her. For a moment she was so astonished that she forgot to be frightened.

"Whoa," she said aloud, the cave picking up her voice

and tossing it back to her from a million directions.

She took a step forward and halted with a scream. The ground in front of her had disappeared and she found herself teetering on the edge of a cliff. Looking down, all she could see was darkness punctured by deadly stalagmites reaching towards her, sharp and lethal. Her cry echoed around her, as though the cave were full of birds. It was only when she saw the pinprick of her torch shining up from the darkness that she realised what she was looking at. She took a tiny step back and picked up a stone. She dropped it in front of her, her breath spilling out in relieved giggles. The pebble dropped with a click, rippling the darkness in front of her. It was just a pool of still water, as smooth and reflective as a mirror.

The cave was still ringing with her scream and she frowned as the echoes bounced around her. It sounded like there was another voice layered over hers as she yelled. She strained her ears but it was impossible to unpick the layers of sound. Her heart quickened again.

"Hello?" she called, caught halfway between feeling

silly and terrified. "Is someone there?"

Nothing. Just her own voice calling back to her. But then came a sound. A tiny scraping noise, pebbles hitting the ground. She froze, sure this was the first murmurings of a rockfall and the cave was about to collapse on her. The sound rose again behind her and she swung round, pointing frantically with the beam of her torch. She caught a flash of movement in the light and stopped. A thin shower of sand and pebbles skittered down the wall of the cave. She followed the stream upwards with her torch, almost screaming again as it picked out something white and luminous against the dark rocks.

It was the face of a boy.

Thirteen

Freya barely had time to process what she was seeing before the boy turned and sprang away from her.

"Hey!" she yelled. "Wait!"

She scrambled up the rocks towards him, just catching his receding form in the light of her torch. He moved like a mountain goat on the rough surface, bouncing confidently from rock to rock, scrambling over ridges and sharp edges with ease.

Freya struggled to keep up with him. What if he was a ghost? He certainly looked the part: pale, gaunt face, eyes shadowed in the hollows of their sockets. But he seemed more afraid of her than she was of him. Maybe ghosts were like spiders in that way.

"Wait, come back!" yelled Freya again. "I'm not going to hurt you."

"Go away," came a voice.

It sounded like it was nearby. The boy's footsteps had stopped.

Freya stood as still as she could, ears straining against the silence.

"I only want to talk to you," she called.

There was no reply. She took a tentative step forward, sweeping the light methodically in front of her.

"Well, I don't want to talk to you. Get out of my cave."

"Your cave? Are—?" She stopped, chewing on her lip. "Are you a ghost?"

A scoff. "Yeah. That's right. I'm a ghost. So you'd better get out of here before I haunt you forever."

Freya planted her hands on her hips. "I don't think

you're a ghost at all."

A ghostly moan echoed out towards Freya, a laugh barely concealed in it. She ran forward a few steps, swinging the torch round a big rock in front of her. The boy was crouched behind it.

"I've seen you before," she said.

The face was a little grubbier, but now that she could see him properly, she was sure. It was the boy who had stolen the pastries outside the bakery. The one who had been following her.

"You were following me."

The boy shook his head. "I literally don't even know who you are."

"I saw you."

"And you shall see me again in your nightmares if you don't goooo," he said, waggling his fingertips at her.

Freya picked up a small pebble from the ground and whipped it at him. It struck him in the chest with a small whack. He scowled, rubbing his chest with the heel of one hand.

"Ow, what was that for?"

Freya shrugged. "To establish that you're not a ghost."

"Fine. I'm not a ghost. But I still don't want to talk to you, so go away." He made a shooing motion at her and turned away.

Now that she was sure he wasn't a ghost, she marched confidently after him. "What are you doing in this cave?"

"Learning to horse-ride," he said.

"What?"

He sighed deeply. "Never mind. What are you doing in this cave?"

"I heard strange noises, so I decided to investigate." She hitched her torch into her other hand. "I'm pretty brave like that," she said, as nonchalantly as she could manage.

"Noises?"

"Yeah. Must have been you. If you were trying to be sneaky, you're not very good at it."

The boy tutted. "Maybe it wasn't me. Maybe it was all the ghosts."

"I haven't seen any ghosts. Just you."

"Well, you wouldn't see ghosts, would you? They're invisible."

Freya huffed. "They are not invisible. Just sort of see-through."

"They are too invisible."

"Are not."

"Is this what you wanted to talk to me about?"

"Of course not." Freya walked along beside him quietly for a while. "You didn't answer my question."

"What question?"

"What are you doing in the cave? I told you what I was doing here. Your turn."

The boy stopped suddenly, Freya running into the back of him. He gestured in front of him. Freya pointed her torch into the space. They had come to a little alcove. In the middle were the charred remains of a fire. There was a raggedy sleeping bag, several melted candle stubs and lots of rubbish. Freya tilted her head to one side. The rubbish was mostly chocolate bar wrappers and mouldering banana skins. She turned back to the boy in astonishment.

"Are you sleeping here?"

He shrugged. "Might be."

"But it's February."

"Thanks, genius. I know that already."

"You'll freeze."

He shrugged again. "Hasn't killed me yet."

"Don't you have somewhere else to go?"

The boy didn't answer; he just kicked at the charred wood, sending a spiral of ash into the air. Freya looked at him more closely. Under the dirt, his face was thin, his lips chapped. His hands were almost purple and spidered with tiny broken veins. There was a hole in the toe of one of his shoes.

He scowled at her. "Take a picture – it'll last longer," he snapped.

"Sorry," said Freya reflexively. She dropped her gaze, fiddling with her torch.

The boy prodded sullenly at the ash pile.

"Listen," she said, "I don't think you should sleep here. It's not safe."

"I'm fine."

"I don't think you are. Why don't you come home with me?"

The boy laughed. "Haven't you ever heard of stranger danger? What if you're an axe murderer? Going with you could be way less safe than sleeping in a cave."

Freya frowned. "Me? You're the one who's been following me. You're more likely to be an axe murderer than I am."

The boy leaned against the wall and raised an eyebrow at her. "I haven't been following you. And I don't need your help. Besides, don't you think your parents would notice if you brought a stray home?"

"My parents are dead," said Freya. It wasn't what she had meant to say and the words caught her by surprise. She almost never talked about it. It never seemed like the kind of thing people wanted to talk about.

"Oh," said the boy, looking at her properly for the first time. "Mine too."

"Oh."

An awkward silence fell. Freya had never met another orphan before. Mostly kids reared away from her when she mentioned it, as though tragedy might be contagious. Or they'd start gushing about how brave she was. She eyed the boy. He wasn't looking at her like he thought she was brave. He still just looked vaguely annoyed. For some reason this was comforting.

"Look," she said, "I live in the B&B in town with my granny. There are a ton of empty rooms, plenty of food, hot water for a bath."

The scowl on the boy's face told her that her final point maybe hadn't been as tactful as she'd hoped.

"You don't need to talk to me if you don't want," she said, "but don't stay here."

The boy didn't say anything; he just shoved himself off the wall and mooched towards her as though he was doing her an enormous favour. Freya understood that this was probably all the thanks she was going to get.

"I'm Freya," she said, pointing her torch back towards the entrance of the cave.

The boy was quiet for a long time. "Teddy," he said finally. "I'm Teddy."

Fourteen

On the walk back to the B&B, Freya's suggestion that they tell her Granny Kate about Teddy had sent him bolting back towards the cave. Freya had to grab his arm to stop him running.

"You don't need to be scared of her. She won't tell anyone you're here."

"She will," said Teddy. "Grown-ups always tell. And then they'll pack me back to the children's home."

Freya's brow creased. There was ice in his voice as he said "children's home". Seeing the expression on his face, she didn't want him to go back there either.

And she couldn't let him go back to the cave. Not in February.

"OK, fine," she said. "No grown-ups."

She managed to sneak Teddy into the B&B without too much trouble. The good thing about living in such an old building was that unexpected noises were pretty standard. Doors creaking in their lopsided frames, pipes clanging in the walls. Granny Kate was unlikely to notice someone else unless she literally tripped over him. Freya grabbed the master key, which could open any door in the B&B, and took him up the back stairs.

"Here you go," she said, pushing the door open. "It's not the fanciest place in the world but it's a heck of a lot nicer than sleeping in a cave."

Teddy pursed his lips. "I suppose."

He went to sit on the bed but stopped short, his eyes darting over the white sheets. Freya caught him glancing down at his filthy hands.

"Why don't I get us something to eat? You must be starving."

Teddy shrugged but his stomach betrayed him,

growling loudly. Freya pretended she didn't notice. She reached into the tall wardrobe and pulled out two fluffy towels. She tossed them on to the bed.

"In case you need them. Bathroom is through that door behind you. I'll be back in a bit."

Teddy grunted. She turned and clicked the door closed, leaving him to it. She made her way down to reception and peeked her head into the breakfast room. No sign of Ms Oleander or Granny Kate. She headed for the kitchen.

She had started to make a ham and cheese sandwich and then remembered the vaguely blue tinge to Teddy's skin. Who knew how long he'd been sleeping in the cold or when he'd last had something hot to eat. She slathered the outside of the sandwich in butter and fired it into the frying pan to make toasties instead. She made two toasties for Teddy and one for herself. She wrapped them in foil to keep them hot. She put a pot of tomato soup on the hob and turned to boil the kettle while it heated. Once the soup was bubbling, she poured it into two bowls. Thinking of Teddy's gaunt face and skinny wrists, she added a generous swirl of cream to each. She arranged the food and a pot of tea on to one of Granny Kate's breakfast trays, adding a packet of bourbon biscuits, two apples and a big jug of orange juice. Clinking as she went, she carried the tray carefully up the stairs.

She had been gone about twenty minutes, which she hoped had given Teddy plenty of time to get cleaned up. She didn't want to hang about in the kitchen too long for fear of Granny Kate coming back and wondering why she needed two bowls of soup and three sandwiches for tea.

She reached the door and realised she had no hands left to knock. She balanced the tray against her tummy and banged her forehead gently against the door.

"Yeah, you can come in," said Teddy.

Freya rolled her eyes. "My hands are full," she shouted through the door. "You have to open it."

There was a moment of silence, followed by the squeak of bedsprings and a dragging sound as Teddy pulled open the door. His eyes lit up as he saw the tray of food before he carefully arranged his features back into a bored expression.

Freya set the tray on the little desk. "I wasn't sure what you liked, so I just made a bit of a mixture. There's ham in the toasties; sorry, I should have asked if you were a vegetarian."

Teddy shook his head. "I'm not."

"Oh, good." Freya picked up a toastie and gestured to the tray. "Tuck in."

Teddy picked up a toastie triangle, dredged it through the soup and took a tentative nibble, his eyes suspiciously on Freya. She deliberately didn't look at him, nibbling her way round the crispy ham sticking out of the crusts of her toastie. He closed his eyes as the food hit his tongue. He dunked the toastie in the soup again, his fingers submerging almost to his knuckle, and shoved the rest of the triangle into his mouth. He hadn't even swallowed it before doing the same with his second triangle.

"Careful," said Freya. "You'll make yourself sick."

She omitted mentioning that this was how she ate basically all the time, and that it was usually

Granny Kate saying this to her. Teddy didn't even look up at her, just kept shovelling food into his mouth. It seemed that until he finished eating, she didn't exist. She took the opportunity to get a better look at him.

Now that Teddy's face was clean, the freckles stood out dark and orange, clashing with his red hair. His hair had gone soft and springy in the shower, curling gently to his collarbone, the strands on top of his head coiling towards the sky. He had slung his damp jacket over the radiator, where it was now steaming gently. He was so focused on his food that he'd stopped scowling. It made him look younger. Freya helped herself to a biscuit.

"How old are you, Teddy?"

"Sixteen," he said round a mouthful of sandwich.

Freya raised an eyebrow.

He started scowling again. He swallowed. "Fine. Fourteen."

"I'm twelve," said Freya.

"I didn't ask."

"I just thought you might like some conversation

with your meal."

"I wouldn't."

"Lots of people do."

"I don't."

Freya sighed and reached for another biscuit. "Fine. We'll just sit here in silence then."

"Fine."

"Fine."

"Good."

Freya jumped as the door to the B&B opened underneath them. She scooted off the bed and leaned over the banister. She groaned. It was Ms Oleander. She was carrying an enormous box, her phone wedged under her chin.

Freya ducked back over the banister before she could be spotted.

"Nothing to worry about," she said to Teddy. "It's just the other guest at the B&B. She's at the other end of the corridor, though, so you won't run into each other."

Whoever was on the other end of the phone had clearly done something to rub Ms Oleander up the wrong way. Her voice floated up the stairs to them, as loud and sharp as a rap on the door. Teddy reared up like a scalded cat, his face turning ashy beneath his freckles.

Freya took a step towards him. "What's wrong?"

"I need to get out of here," he said.

"What?"

"I need to leave. Right now."

"What are you talking about?"

Teddy scrambled off the bed, upending a glass of orange juice in his hurry. He winced as the stain spread across the white bedspread.

"Oh god, I'm sorry," he said, running to the bathroom and returning with a handful of toilet paper. He dabbed ineffectually at the stain, grimacing as the tissue disintegrated.

"Leave it, don't worry about that. We're a B&B; we've cleaned up worse stains than that."

"Again with the axe murderer vibes," he said, almost with a smile.

He grabbed the packet of biscuits and shoved them into his pocket. "Listen, thanks for feeding me. It was nice of you. But I have to go."

The insistent rhythm of Ms Oleander's voice sounded once more. Teddy winced and yanked his jacket from the radiator. He shoved an arm into it, wriggling with pleasure at the warm material.

Freya turned towards the door and back towards Teddy. "Wait. It's because of her, isn't it?" she said, her eyes growing wide.

"I don't know what you're talking about," said Teddy, looking down.

Freya threw the door closed and leaned her weight against it, her arms folded.

"That night outside the town hall," she said, "you weren't watching me at all. You were watching Ms Oleander. You know her."

"I will physically move you if I have to."

"That is not an answer to my question."

Teddy looked desperately unhappy.

Freya sat down cross-legged in front of the door and focused on making herself as heavy as possible just in case he did try to lift her.

"Spill," she said.

Teddy didn't look any less keen to leave but he did slump back on to the bed. He threw one hand up. "OK, fine. Yes, I know her."

"Is she the reason that you're in Edge?"

"Sort of."

"If you don't start talking, I'm going to start throwing things."

He held up his palm. "All right! I worked for her back in the city. The children's home I lived in has this programme where they hook kids up with local business people. It's supposed to be a mentoring thing."

"OK. That sounds … good, I guess?" said Freya.

Teddy scoffed. "In theory, yeah. But most of the businesses just use it to get workers they don't have to pay."

Freya wrinkled her nose. "That's horrible. And that's what Ms Oleander did?"

Teddy grunted.

"And you worked with her on her Edge boardwalk project?"

Another grunt. Freya tugged off a boot and threw

it at him, a bit harder than she'd intended. It hit his shin with a clatter.

"Ow!"

"I'm sorry! Well, I'm not that sorry, I did warn you. But I'm sorry for throwing something heavy. Come on, you were working with Ms Oleander and...?"

Teddy swallowed. "Yeah, I was working on this project with her. A little seaside town where she wanted to buy up some property for development."

Freya drummed her fingers on the carpet. "Yeah, I know that bit. So what happened? Why are you living in a cave on the beach instead of at the B&B with her?"

"She doesn't know I'm here," said Teddy. "I followed her."

"Because you're secretly in love with her?"

"Oh, gross! Absolutely not!"

"Well, if you don't hurry up and tell me, I'm just going to keep taking wild guesses."

Teddy sighed. "Most of the stuff I was doing for her was pretty boring. Making copies of documents.

Getting her tea. Stuff like that. So I started snooping around."

Freya nodded approvingly. "And you found...?"

"I found out why she really wants to buy the boardwalk."

"So she can knock down everything that's here and build luxury retail space, whatever that means," said Freya.

Teddy shook his head vehemently. "That's just a cover. It's a lie. She's not interested in what's on top of the boardwalk. She's after what's underneath it." He paused.

Freya considered throwing her other boot at him. "Which is?"

He looked up at her, his eyes enormous. "Treasure."

Fifteen

"Treasure," breathed Freya.

"People have found it before," said Teddy defensively.

Freya shook her head. "No, I believe you." She thought of Lin and their treasure hunts and something ached hard inside her. She pushed her glasses up her nose. "I believe you. So you found out she was looking for treasure. Then what?"

"There are laws about what happens when someone finds treasure. It happens more often than you think."

Freya raised an eyebrow.

"OK, not that often. But it happens."

"All right. So what are the laws?"

"It gets split evenly between whoever finds it and whoever owns the land. She's planning to be both of those people. But if I find it before her, I get half."

Freya blew out a long, low whistle. "She'd be furious."

Teddy shrugged. "Not much she could do about it."

Freya thought about this for a moment, then sat bolt upright. "Wait, so what happens if you were to find it before she buys the land?"

"I don't care. I still get my half."

Freya stood up and went to sit beside him on the bed. "I care. If we found the treasure before Ms Oleander buys the land, the town would have the right to half of it."

Teddy leaned away from her. "I don't like that 'we'."

Freya shuffled close to him again. "Tough. Because we're a 'we' now."

Teddy stood up and paced to the other side of the room. "No way. I don't need some kid trailing around after me getting in the way. Besides, I'm not sharing my half. I don't know how much is down there and I need enough to make sure I never have to go back to the children's home."

"Firstly, I'm basically one year younger than you, so you can knock off calling me a 'kid'." Freya sat for a moment, her brain ticking. "And I could come in useful. I can build things; that could be handy. And I've lived here my whole life. I know the caves better than you possibly could." This wasn't technically true, but Teddy didn't need to know that.

He blinked across at her, his brow furrowed. She could tell that she hadn't quite managed to sell it.

"And," she said, "I'm not interested in your half of the treasure. You can keep it. As long as the town gets their half."

Teddy pursed his lips. "Fine. But if you get hurt, it's on you. I'm out for the treasure, nothing else."

Freya's brain was fizzing. She had no idea how much money Ms Oleander had offered the council for the boardwalk. But if it was all a ploy to get at what was underneath, the treasure had to be worth more. Lots more. With even half of it, the town would be able to send Ms Oleander packing and save the boardwalk. She could have danced. But she fought to keep her features under control. She had the feeling that looking too happy might cause Teddy to change his mind.

"Deal," she said, holding out her hand for a handshake. Teddy just stared at her. She sighed and dropped it. "So what was your plan? Obviously you haven't managed to find it yet."

Teddy shook his head. "I copied all her maps and documents for her. So I tried to draw up everything I could remember, and I've been working off that."

Freya hummed softly. "Memory is a funny thing. It's hard to remember exact pictures."

"Clearly," said Teddy. "But unless you have a better idea, my memory is all we've got."

Freya shoved her hands in her pockets and sighed. She brightened as her hand closed round something small and heavy. "Actually, I do have a better idea."

She held out the object in her hand. It was the master key for the B&B.

They waited until they heard Ms Oleander leaving again and headed down the corridor to her room. A flutter of nerves rolled through Freya.

"Come on, come on," said Teddy, bouncing on the balls of his feet. "Let's go."

Freya took a deep breath, turned the key and pushed the door open. The room was fastidiously tidy. It almost looked as though no one was staying there at all. Freya pulled the door closed and locked it behind them. The air smelled faintly of violets, sweet and cloying. She suppressed a sneeze.

Teddy shoved his hands in his pockets and shifted his weight uncomfortably. "Where do we start?"

"I don't know. I've never searched someone's room before."

"And you think I have? It's your B&B. And your plan. I thought you might have some ideas."

Freya pushed her glasses up her nose. "All right, all right. I'll check the wardrobe. You check under the bed."

Freya pulled open the door of the cupboard. The smell of violets hit her again, stronger this time.

The wardrobe was filled with clothes, neatly ironed and hanging in coloured groups. She frowned as she started to pat down the silken dresses. "Who actually uses the wardrobe in a hotel? I thought everyone just lived out of a suitcase."

"Speaking of," said Teddy. "Come and help me with this."

He was halfway under the bed, his wiggling legs sticking out.

Freya got on to her belly on the floor beside him and peered under the bed at Ms Oleander's suitcase, the one Freya had hauled up the stairs on the day she arrived. Teddy had one hand round the handle. Freya did the same, using her other hand to drag herself backwards. She'd never been crazy about small spaces and the bed felt like it was pressing down on top of her. She wriggled on the carpet, moving an agonising centimetre at a time. Teddy grunted beside her. Eventually the case was close enough to the edge of the bed that they were able to sit on the floor, plant their feet on the bedframe and use that leverage to slide it out.

Teddy flopped on to his back, panting.

Freya dug him in the stomach. "No time for that," she said, gesturing impatiently at the combination padlock on the case. "Any ideas?"

Teddy scrunched up his face and thought hard. He took the lock in his hand, spinning the numbers. He carefully clicked the wheels until the lock read "313" and gave it a yank. Nothing happened. He hissed in frustration.

This time Freya flopped on to her back. "Well, that was worthwhile."

"Give me a minute," he said, closing his eyes.

After a moment, he looked back down at the lock and used his fingernail to click the wheel round one more number. 314. The padlock sprang open. He gave a delighted whoop, which was smothered by Freya clapping a hand over his mouth.

He shoved her away. "She's gone out," he said sullenly.

"Yeah, but my Granny Kate is still downstairs. I don't want her wondering who's making noise up in Ms Oleander's room."

Teddy smirked. "You could just tell her I'm a ghost."

"You're so funny," said Freya. "Come on, let's see what she's got locked in here."

They unbuckled the heavy case and heaved it open.

"Jackpot," breathed Freya.

Stacks of documents arranged in neat bundles. Maps of Edge, drawings of the boardwalk, sketches of the new development.

"We have to be careful," said Freya. "Everything has to go back exactly where it was." She pulled her phone from her pocket, stood up and took a photograph. "So we can remember what it looked like when we opened it," she explained.

"Smart," said Teddy, nodding. He caught Freya's surprised look and rolled his eyes. "All right, get over it. Even a stopped clock is right twice a day."

Freya huffed and sat back down. She removed the first bundle of documents from the case, pulling off the elastic and shuffling through it.

"It's hard to tell what's useful and what isn't," she said, squinting at a page covered in numbers.

"Then we'd better take photos of everything."

They worked their way methodically through the files. They had no idea when Ms Oleander would be back, so they moved as quickly as they could, checking each photo to make sure it wasn't blurry before moving on to the next. As she snapped, Freya would pass each file back to Teddy, who would re-bundle them and set them to one side, ready to go back in the case.

"Thank goodness," said Freya, when they could see the bottom of the case. She stretched her arms above her head, her back giving a satisfying click as it straightened out. As her hands came back down, one of her wrists collided with the point of the pencil she had wound into her hair. She pressed her hand to her mouth. No blood. Good. Blood made her queasy.

She pulled the pencil out of her hair, bringing it falling down around her face. She tugged it back, twisted it into a knot and went to shove the pencil back through to hold it in place. Then she had an idea. She grabbed a stack of papers from Teddy's pile.

"Careful!" said Teddy. "What are you doing?"

Freya flipped through the pile until she reached

a map of the coast dotted with lines and the occasional arrow.

"We have photos of all this, right?" she said.

"Yeah, unless you messed something up."

"Right," she said with a grin, "so there's no reason to make things easy for her."

She erased a number of the dotted lines, pencilling them back in in completely different places.

Teddy grinned back at her. "I never thought I'd say this," he said, "but I like the way you think."

They both laughed. They started to slot the documents back into the case, changing Ms Oleander's maps anywhere they could. They were so absorbed in their task that they didn't hear the footsteps until they hit the hallway outside. Freya's eyes widened in panic, mirrored in Teddy's stricken face. She swivelled round, used both legs to boot the case back under the bed and dragged herself underneath with it. Teddy was only a second behind her, swinging his feet under the bed just as the key turned in the lock.

Freya clapped a hand over her mouth to muffle the sound of her breathing as Ms Oleander entered the room. Beside her Teddy tensed as Ms Oleander's patent-leather shoes came into view, only a few centimetres from their noses. Freya wished she could roll on to her back but there wasn't space. There was barely room for the two of them to fit at all. Teddy was curled round the case, one arm trapped under himself at an awkward angle. He was grimacing in discomfort but seemed to be putting all his concentration into breathing as slowly and shallowly as he could.

"Hello?" said Ms Oleander.

Freya's heart slammed into her ribs in fright. Teddy's knuckles were white on top of the case.

Then Ms Oleander said, "Yes, it's me."

Freya's eyes went blurry with relief. She felt Teddy loosen beside her. Ms Oleander was on the phone.

"That's right," she said. "Everything's in place."

There was a pause as the person on the other end said something. Freya strained her ears but she could only hear the faint buzz of their voice. It was impossible to make out what they were saying.

Ms Oleander laughed: a cold, unpleasant sound. "No,

they have no idea. They were practically begging me to take it off their hands."

A thrill of anger ran down Freya's spine. She clenched her fists and her teeth.

More murmuring from the voice on the other end of the phone.

"No problem. As soon as the sale goes through, we tear down what's here and start digging."

A few seconds of silence.

"OK, I'll speak to you soon."

There was a small beep as Ms Oleander ended the call. She sighed happily and fell back on to the bed. The bedsprings gave a loud screech and Freya winced as the mattress dropped several more centimetres. Teddy caught her eye, giving her a "what now?" look. Freya had no idea. As far as she could tell, they had no option but to stay exactly where they were. She had a horrible vision of being trapped under the bed for the entire night. Closing her eyes helped a little, she didn't feel so stuck then, but she was terrified that she'd fall asleep. Ms Oleander's nails clacked against the screen of her phone, the mattress giving

another agonised groan every time she shifted on
the bed.

* * *

Freya had no idea how long they'd been under the
bed. She didn't dare reach for her phone in case
the sound or the light gave them away. She clapped
a hand over her mouth to stifle a gasp as Ms
Oleander's shoes swung back into sight. She grimaced.
Who put their shoes on the bed?

Ms Oleander wandered back and forth across the
room, humming gently to herself. Freya was suddenly
seized with panic that she'd go for her case and see
them. But to Freya's undying relief she headed for the
bathroom. Freya held her breath as the lock clicked.
The sound of the shower running followed shortly
after.

She nudged Teddy and gave him a nod. *Now.* They
scrambled out from under the bed as quietly as they
could, running on tiptoes for the door. Freya eased
the handle down, muffling its click as best she could.
She pulled it gently closed behind her. The sound
of running water disappeared. Freya couldn't tell

whether it had stopped or whether the door was blocking it, but either way, they turned on their heels and fled, and didn't stop until they reached Teddy's room.

Sixteen

Every evening after school that week, Freya and Teddy would pore over the maps they'd found. With the sun still setting around five o'clock, it was too dark to go exploring the caves. And if they had to wait until Saturday, they wanted to be ready.

It seemed like Ms Oleander had a pretty good idea of where the treasure was supposed to be. She had circled a specific cave on one map, although the town itself was peppered with question marks. She obviously didn't know whether any of the town's smuggling tunnels would lead to the right cave.

"No wonder she was poking around our basement," said Freya. "She must have been looking for tunnels."

"Well, she needn't have bothered," said Teddy. "I went snooping around there the first day you were at school, and all I found was a bunch of old Christmas decorations."

"And I suppose she doesn't need to bother now if she's going to tear the whole boardwalk down. She's just waiting for her chance to start digging."

Granny Kate was out, so they had moved to Freya's bedroom, which had a bigger desk. She watched Teddy take in her sketches and inventions and try very hard not to look impressed. They cross-referenced the maps with photographs Freya had taken of the beach and the caves Teddy had searched before Freya had found him. He was bent over Freya's phone, a pencil stuck behind his ear, a crease of concentration between his eyebrows.

"Do you really think there could be a load of treasure buried right under our feet?" asked Freya.

He looked up at her. "Yeah, why not? Don't you?"

"I don't know," said Freya, scratching her chin with

the end of her pencil. "It sounds so ridiculous. Buried treasure. Like something from a movie."

"Is there a 'but' coming or are you talking yourself out of the idea?"

Freya shook her head. "No, definitely not. There were pirates here. Everyone knows that. And it wouldn't be the first time a grown-up has come to Edge and done something mad in search of buried treasure."

Teddy nodded. "The thing with the diamond. I heard about that."

Freya leaned over her desk and rearranged the pieces of her puzzle box. She popped the lid open.

"We found this once, not too long ago. Tell me that doesn't look like treasure."

She flipped the coin she and Lin had found at him with her thumb. It turned in the air, catching the light.

Teddy caught it. He traced its patterns with a fingertip. "Is it real gold?"

Freya shrugged. "I think so. I looked up how to test if gold was real and it said if it was fake, vinegar would make it change colour."

"That's cool. And it didn't?"

"Nope. Not that I could see anyway."

"Do you bite it? I've seen people do that."

"What would that achieve?"

"I have no idea. I've just seen people do it."

"Well, you're not biting it. Give it back."

Teddy held up the coin between his fingers. "I won't bite it. So you don't know if it's valuable?"

"Nope. I want to keep it anyway. Some things are too lovely to sell."

Teddy nodded and was quiet for a moment. He handed the coin back to Freya. It was warm from his palm.

"That's a pretty good spot," he said. "Maybe you have a nose for treasure."

Freya laughed. "I've got something better than that. I have a metal detector." She clamped her mouth shut, too late.

Teddy's head jerked up. "Why am I only hearing about this now?"

Freya dropped her gaze.

"Didn't you think a metal detector would be helpful in finding a big pile of treasure? Isn't that literally what people buy metal detectors for?"

Freya shrugged. "Well, I don't really have it right now anyway."

"What do you mean? Where is it?"

"Someone else has it."

Teddy raised his eyebrows, waiting for her to elaborate.

Freya dug dents into the wooden surface of her desk with her thumbnail.

"Who borrows a metal detector?" Teddy said. "It's weird enough to have a metal detector in the first place."

"Just this girl. We bought it together. It's over at her house."

"OK. So let's go get it."

Freya sighed deeply. "It's not that simple."

"Uh, yes it is. We need it, she has it, we go and get it."

Freya did a full-body eye-roll. "Fine. But *I'll* go and get it. You stay here."

Teddy sat up. "Why?"

"Would you relax? I'm not planning to go without

153

you. Things are just a little sticky with the girl who has it, that's all."

Teddy yawned pointedly.

Freya's insides fizzed as she jammed her boots on to her feet. "I won't be long," she said, grabbing her coat from the hook on the back of her door. "If I go now, I can be back before dark. Don't touch my inventing stuff. There's a system and you'll mess it up."

Teddy tried to look as though her inventing stuff was the most boring thing he could possibly imagine but there was a flicker in his eyes that made her think he was absolutely going to touch all of it.

She collided unexpectedly with Granny Kate in reception.

"Oh!" said Granny Kate. "I thought you were out."

"I'm just going. I actually thought you were out," retorted Freya.

"Well, I was. For a few minutes. I popped round to the bakery."

Freya took in the plate in Granny Kate's hands, carefully arranged with cream buns and little triangle sandwiches. She raised an eyebrow.

"That's a bit fancy for tea," she said. "Not like you to eat two cakes."

Granny Kate turned very pink and adopted a haughty expression. "They're not both for me."

"Oh?" Freya's face darkened. "You'd better not be about to tell me that you're buying cream cakes for Ms Oleander."

"Of course not! I do have friends of my own, you know."

Freya put her hands on her hips. "Oh really? Like who?"

"I don't demand to know what you're doing with all your friends," said Granny Kate.

Freya raised an eyebrow. She hadn't actually been that interested to start with. She'd mostly been asking to gauge whether there would be a cream bun going spare. But she was definitely interested now.

"Uh, yes you do actually," said Freya.

Granny Kate turned even more pink. "Well, Mr Bajwa mentioned that he might stop by if he was passing."

Freya bit down on a grin. "Oh, did he?"

"There's no need to look at me like that. It's perfectly ordinary for me to have a friend drop by."

"Of course. Which is why you're wearing lipstick."

Granny Kate bumped Freya out of the way with one hip. "That is quite enough out of you. Go on, get wherever you're going and give me some peace."

Freya managed to hold her laughter until she was out of sight and then fell into helpless giggles. The wind had all its usual bite as she opened the door of the B&B but her heart lifted as she started down the road and saw that the first green daffodils had started to raise their heads from the flower beds. They always delighted her, a riot of yellow sunshine after what felt like the darkest month.

One year the snow had got so bad in early March that the town was completely cut off. Freya remembered Granny Kate coming home from the supermarket, her arms full of daffodils and yelling, "There was no bread in the shop, but *look*!" The flowers were a reminder that spring was just round the corner, that the town would soon start creaking back into life. Although who knew what that would look like this year. If Ms Oleander got her way, the boardwalk would be torn up by the time summer arrived.

The thoughts of spring were shoved from her head as she approached Lin's door. She steeled herself, pushed through the gate and, after a moment's hesitation, rang the doorbell. Even that felt strange. She'd become such a part of the furniture at Lin's house that she normally went straight round to the back door, announcing herself with a shout once she was inside. Maybe Lin's mother would answer, or Mei, and then she could just get the detector and go without having to see—

Lin opened the door, her mouth falling into a neat "o" as she saw Freya standing on the doorstep. Her face broke in a smile that hurt Freya's insides to look at.

"Freya, thank goodness," she gushed. "I didn't know whether I should keep calling or whether that was even more annoying and I should give you some space. I just—"

"I'm not coming in. I just want the metal detector."

Lin's smile cracked. "Oh. Are you—"

"I don't want to talk to you," said Freya. Although, all of a sudden, she did. She desperately wanted to talk to her. She desperately wanted to tell her about Teddy and the treasure and the fact that her Granny Kate was buying clandestine cream buns for Harpreet's grandpa.

"Can we please just—"

"No," said Freya firmly. "No, we can't."

Lin turned one of her feet on its side, her weight on one bent ankle. "Mei is organising a protest," she said, "the day the sale goes through. A last attempt to convince the council to change their mind. It's a bit noisier than a petition, so she's hoping it'll be harder to ignore."

"Whatever," said Freya.

"I was just thinking that maybe we could—"

Freya spotted the metal detector leaning in the porch behind Lin. She reached behind her, grabbed it and ran back down the path before the tears gathering in her eyes had a chance to fall. She ran, ignoring Lin's shouts behind her, until she was out of sight by the sea wall. She sat down on the wall and cried. The tear tracks on her face stung in the cold, her nose hurt and the whole thing was so pathetic that it made her cry harder.

"Freya?"

Freya straightened up and found herself looking into the face of Ms Oleander. She wiped her nose hastily on her sleeve.

"What's going on?" asked Ms Oleander.

"You mean other than the fact that I'm going to lose my home in a week?" Freya blinked tears away.

Ms Oleander closed her eyes, as though she found the whole conversation distasteful. When she opened them again, her brisk customer-service smile had been reapplied. She nodded at the metal detector in Freya's arms by way of changing the subject. "That's quite a contraption. What are you up to with that?"

Freya smiled sweetly. "Treasure hunting."

And, with that, she turned and headed back towards the B&B, laughing at the look on Ms Oleander's face.

Seventeen

On Saturday morning Freya and Teddy set off early, dragging themselves out of bed with the sun. The streets were quiet, the beach completely deserted. Freya hoisted the metal detector on to one shoulder and hopped down on to the sand. Waves of fog rolled in off the sea. Freya felt as though she was walking through the clouds. As the fog obscured the beach in front of them, they continued walking, taking tiny steps with their hands outstretched. It made for a strange experience, as though the beach was blinking in and out of existence in front of them.

Their footsteps splashed quietly.

Teddy stopped suddenly. "I think there's someone following us," he whispered.

Freya turned to look behind them but she couldn't see anything, just the shifting fog. She shook herself and pressed forward. "It's just echoes," she said, her ears tuning in to the sound of footsteps falling a second after their own.

But the longer they walked, the less sure she was. She could feel the prickle of eyes on the back of her neck. She reminded herself of all the times she'd felt like this, all the times she'd been convinced that something terrible was watching her. It was only her imagination.

There was a small *oof* from behind them, the sound of something soft colliding with a rock, and Freya jumped about a mile in the air. Teddy leapt into the fog and came up brandishing someone by the collar.

"I told you someone was following us! Ms Oleander must have sent a spy!"

Freya groaned. "She's not a spy. Lin, what are you doing?"

Lin shook herself free indignantly. "What am *I* doing? What are you doing? Wandering about the beach in the fog. You're basically asking to fall in the sea." She perked up. "Wait, Ms Oleander? Did you find something?"

Freya pressed her lips into a stubborn line.

Teddy looked between them. "And who are you?"

Lin planted her hands on her hips. "Who am I? Who are you?"

"Are you going to turn every question I ask round on me? Because that seriously sounds like something a spy would do."

"I don't know," said Lin absolutely straight-faced. "Are *you* going to turn every question I ask round on me?"

Teddy blinked blankly at her, then he grinned. "I like her."

"Well, I don't," said Freya.

Lin's bravado cracked. "Freya, please, can we just talk? I want you to know how sorry I am."

"No," said Freya. "I don't want to talk about it. I'm too hurt."

Teddy moaned. "Can we not do all these feelings right now? We don't have time."

Lin ignored him. "Freya, I'm so sorry. I'm really just so sorry. You were totally right. I was being mean and thoughtless and I just didn't think about how frightened you'd be."

Freya crossed her arms.

Lin took a tentative step towards her. "And then I saw how much of a mistake I'd made and I panicked and said a bunch of horrible stuff that I didn't mean at all. You're my best friend. I've been totally, utterly miserable without you."

Freya felt the poison inside her start to drain away. Teddy looked at her. "You have to admit that was a pretty good apology. Even I feel kinda moved."

Freya looked down, fighting to stop the smile that was spreading over her face. She adopted her most serious expression and fixed it on Lin. "Fine," she said. "I forgive you, you absolute nightmare. But—"

The rest of her speech was swallowed by Lin's puffer jacket as Lin wrapped her in a massive hug.

"Oh my gosh, thank goodness. I've been absolutely

losing my mind," said Lin, squeezing the breath out of Freya.

"OK, warm fuzzy moment over. Well done, everyone," said Teddy. "Now, can we *please* get a move on?"

Freya tugged Lin along, explaining the plan as they walked. The cave the maps seemed to point to was towards the edge of the beach, where the sand petered out to a tiny silver strip between the sea and the jagged cliff edge. If their maps were correct, it would lead them down, away from the sea, deep under the town.

Freya turned to her friends. "Ready?"

"Absolutely not," said Lin.

"Right then. Let's go."

The cave mouth sparkled in the cold morning light, the thin beam of their torch picking out craggy columns bejewelled with frost. Beyond that, the beam disappeared, swallowed into the dark throat of the cave. Lin held the torch, Teddy had the maps and Freya swung the metal detector in front of them, its alien whirring seeming even more bizarre within the quiet blackness. The dark was almost liquid, moving and pulsing around them. Freya's eyes were playing tricks on her, flashes of movement in the corner of her vision sending her spinning, peering into emptiness. Eventually she forced herself to keep her eyes on the pool of light at her feet spilling from Lin's torch.

Their buoyant chatter skittered off the walls around them, bouncing back in strange mocking echoes. After a while, even Lin fell silent. Freya thought the silence was even worse, but she couldn't quite bring herself to break it. The metal detector beeped in front of them and Freya stopped, directing the light from Lin's torch. A copper penny glinted in a tiny pool in front of them. Not quite treasure but Freya slipped it into her pocket all the same. For luck.

She winced as the metal detector collided with something hard. The clang was so fantastic that Lin dropped the torch in fright. The light skittered frantically around, illuminating dark crevices and filling Freya's mind with strange shapes.

"Sorry," she said, bending down to pick up the torch

and handing it back to Lin.

Lin swept the torch upwards. They'd reached what looked like an impassable wall. Freya was glad it was the metal detector that had collided with it and not her face. The rock was black and crusted with sharp barnacles that tore at Freya's skin as she swept her fingertips over its surface. Seawater sprang in little rivulets round slick green swathes of seaweed.

"What now?" asked Lin.

"We must have the wrong cave," said Freya.

"No way," said Teddy. "Bring that torch over here."

Lin obliged without so much as a smart comment. Freya pressed her head in between them and the three of them squinted down at the map.

"This is definitely right," said Teddy. His finger traced a line from the steps on to the beach down to the cliffs they were currently inside. "See? This is where we've come from. And this must be where we are."

"So there must be a way through," said Freya.

"Except there isn't," said Teddy.

"Wait," said Lin, "what's that?"

She was pointing the torch over to the left. There was a dark spot on the wall. Freya's eyes had skimmed right over it because it was so close in colour to the rock around it but now that the torch was pointing straight at it, she could see a gap. She clapped Lin on the back. Occasionally her wandering attention really came in handy.

Freya hoisted the metal detector on to her shoulder and they followed the torchlight to the gap in the wall. It was at about waist height and didn't look quite tall enough to stand up in. The dark inside seemed solid but when Freya stretched her arm inside, she found only empty air. She turned to her friends. They looked less than thrilled.

"Ladies first?" said Teddy.

Lin rolled her eyes, shoved her way between the two of them and hauled herself up into the hole. She couldn't straighten up, so took strange crouching steps like a glitching video-game character. Then she disappeared through the floor, taking the light with her.

Eighteen

The darkness was huge and immediate. Panic slammed into Freya like a train.

"Lin!" she yelled, her hands scrabbling at the wall, looking for the ledge.

"It's OK!" came Lin's voice.

There were a few shuffling, grunting sounds and Lin's head popped back into view. Freya could have fainted with relief, although she wasn't sure whether she was happier to see Lin or the torch.

"It drops," said Lin. "The ground just disappears. I fell through. Don't you do that. Come slowly."

Freya pulled herself up into the gap. "Are you OK? Are you hurt?"

"Nah. Serves me right for pretending to get swallowed by a cave before. I landed a bit weird on my ankle but I can still put weight on it." She reached a hand towards Freya. "You're hurt, though, silly."

Freya looked down. Her palms were speckled with red where they'd scraped against the rocks. She hadn't even noticed, but now they started to smart. She shook her head, blotting the spots of blood on her trousers. "I'm fine."

Lin dropped back down into the hole and pointed the torch upwards so that Freya could see where it was. Teddy passed the metal detector up to her and Freya dragged it behind her, grimacing at the sound of metal against rock. It'd be a miracle if it made it back out of the cave in one piece. Although, she supposed, the same could be true of the three of them. She tried to push that thought away but the harder she pushed, the bigger it became. She heard Teddy clamber through behind her. Having him blocking her exit made her panic rise again, so she gritted her teeth and scrambled forward faster.

When she reached the hole, she sat down, sliding her legs underneath and wincing as the stone bit into her sore palms. She landed on her feet, Lin helping her as she stumbled, then her friend pointed the torch back upwards, lighting Teddy's way as he jumped in. He batted Freya away as she reached out to steady him, and then immediately had to grab for Lin when he lost his footing. Freya turned away so he wouldn't see her giggling.

They were in another huge cavern. The darkness of the rock made it hard to see where it ended. It looked as though it might stretch on forever. It was like floating in space. Freya reached out to touch a piece of rock, to remind herself that she was solid. She tipped her head back to look at the hole they'd come through. She hoped they'd be able to find their way back. She'd thought about tying herself to a piece of string that she could follow back, like Theseus in the Greek myth, but, knowing her luck, she'd end up getting tangled in it or snapping it. A trail of breadcrumbs wasn't much of a goer either outside of the fairy tales. She pulled a piece of yellow chalk from her pocket, stretched on to her tiptoes and drew a bunch of arrows round the hole. They were luminous when Lin shone the torch up at them. She just hoped they'd be enough.

They consulted Teddy's map. The paper was curling in the damp of the cave. They were too deep underground now for their phones to work, so they huddled round the compass Freya had brought. Teddy pulled a pencil from behind his ear and marked out where they'd come so far. They had turned away from the sea and should be standing just about at the border where the beach met the boardwalk. Freya gazed around at the cavernous darkness. She felt like she was in the belly of some enormous creature. So this was what lay at the heart of the town. She crossed her fingers and hoped there was something glittering at its centre.

"I think we want to go this way," said Teddy, pointing.

Lin nodded and pointed her torch in the direction of Teddy's finger. They moved slowly over the uneven ground, Freya stopping every so often to draw another arrow. The ground was pooled with water and slippery. Freya just hoped the arrows would last. In theory, they'd be able to follow Teddy's map, but she'd like to know for sure that they were heading back the way they had come. She tried to ignore the steady downward pitch of the ground.

"Looks like there should be another tunnel," said Teddy. "Check the walls."

They patted the walls and Freya's finger closed round another strange little ledge. This must be it. "Lin, over here."

Lin pointed the torch in the direction of Freya's voice. There was a gap in the rock.

Freya bent to peer inside. "We'll have to crawl," she said, her throat tightening.

"Are we sure this is the way?" asked Lin.

Teddy pointed to the relevant spot on the map. "It looks like the only way we can go."

They patted around for a few more minutes, hoping to find a bigger tunnel, but this was the only gap.

Lin got down on her knees, but Freya put a hand on

her shoulder. "No, you went first last time. I'll go."

"Are you sure?"

Freya had never felt less sure of something in her life. But she wordlessly took the torch from Lin and moved her out of the way. "It doesn't look like it's narrow for too long," she said. "It looks like it opens out again."

She was talking to herself as much as to the others. She jammed the torch between her shoulder and her ear and bent to look down the tunnel. Then, her blood pounding in her throat, she eased herself into the space. With her puffy coat, her shoulders scraped the walls on either side. The tunnel continued on a downward slope and Freya tried not to think about how far they were from the surface, how every step seemed to take them deeper. Her hands splashed into a puddle and she stopped. Lin crawled into the back of her. She reached a tentative hand out, probing the bottom of the puddle. She had horrifying visions of being plunged into a freezing underground pool, of having to duck under the water and grope blindly for the next bit of tunnel. She gritted her teeth and slid her hand further along the ground. There was no drop.

She called back to the others. "The ground is wet up here but it's just a puddle. The water isn't deep."

She shuddered as she crawled through it, her thick trousers sucking up the water and clinging to her legs. She heard Lin cry out in disgust behind her. The tunnel grew narrower, pressing in on her, making it more difficult to keep moving. She was the smallest of the group.

"Do we still have everyone?" she yelled.

"Just about," grunted Teddy from the back.

Freya's glasses slid down her nose and she shoved them back up, hard. She'd seen enough movies to know what happened to the girl who lost her glasses. The tunnel started to ease off and Freya scrambled towards the opening she could see at the end. She burst out into a large open space and leaned against the wall, breathing hard. Lin emerged a few seconds later, with Teddy behind her.

"You OK?" asked Lin.

Freya nodded. "That was a lot."

"It was. You're so brave."

"We're so brave."

Freya raised her arms above her head and stretched out the knots that were gripping her shoulders. "Where to now?"

Teddy put the map on the ground and held out a hand for the torch. He sketched the last bit of their journey in pencil. "So if we're here now –" he pointed – "there should be a series of little caves fanning off this one. And the treasure should be in one of them."

Freya's breath hitched. Were they really about to stumble into a treasure trove?

"OK," she said. "We need a system. Let's do it like a maze. Put your left hand on the wall and don't break contact. In theory, we should do a full loop and end up back where we started."

She bent and drew a huge yellow "X" where they were standing.

"'X' marks the spot," said Lin.

Freya reached out her left hand until her fingertips were brushing the wall. The others followed suit and they started to follow the meandering lines of the cave. Freya squeaked as her hand disappeared into a hole. They had found the first cave. It was much smaller than the ones they'd been in so far. It only took a few moments to sweep the torch around and see that it was empty. They carried on to the next. And the next. And the next.

Freya bit down hard on her bottom lip. "Please, please, please," she whispered, not even really caring if the others could hear her.

The beam of her torch hit on something glowing in front of them. Her heart leapt and then turned to stone. It was their yellow "X". They had come back to where they started. They stopped, staring silently at the "X".

"There's nothing here," said Teddy. He sounded like he might burst into tears. "There's nothing here."

Freya spun round, looking back the way they'd come. "It must be here."

"What, do you think we missed a big sparkly stash of treasure? It's not here. We're in the wrong place."

"That doesn't make any sense," said Lin, grabbing the map. "If we followed the map, we have to be in the right place."

"If we were in the right place, there would be treasure," said Teddy.

Freya sank back against the wall, putting her head in her hands.

"Maybe it got moved," said Lin. "Or someone else got here first. Or maybe the map is wrong."

"Only none of that helps us," said Freya. "If we don't find the treasure, the sale goes through and Ms Oleander wins."

Lin pointed the torch around them. "At least if someone else got here first, Ms Oleander isn't going to get her hands on any treasure either."

"That doesn't make me feel that much better," said Freya. "Then she'll have knocked down my home for nothing."

"Besides," said Teddy, "it's probably just that the map is wrong. If there's treasure down here anywhere, she's bound to find it eventually. She can just dig until she does."

"Well, maybe we can do the same," said Lin.

Freya put a hand on her arm. "No we can't. Even

coming this far would have been impossible without the map. There's no way we can go looking around tunnels without some kind of guide."

"That can't just be it," said Lin.

"Well, it is," snapped Teddy. His face was luminous in the torchlight, freckles standing out dark against his grey skin.

He turned away from them and started to crawl back the way they'd come, not even bothering to wait for the torch.

Nineteen

Almost immediately after getting home from the beach, Freya started to feel funny. She wasn't sure whether it was all the cavorting about in freezing caves that had done it or whether everything was just getting on top of her, but for the first time in a long time she found herself really, properly sick.

Her temperature spiked, leaving her shivering in cold sweats. Her throat felt like it had been filled with hot glass. She started to see fuzzy spots in her vision when she stood up for too long. She pushed a note under Teddy's door, telling him to help himself to anything in the kitchen and took to bed, wrapping herself round a hot-water bottle like a squid. Granny Kate fussed around with blankets and cold cloths for her forehead, while Lin called in with magic soup and updates on Mei's protest. Their kitchen had become a hive of activity, people painting banners and handing out stickers. Freya stayed as still and quiet as she could, willing herself to get better in time to attend.

But one day passed, then another, and before Freya knew it, it was Saturday again. They were almost out of time. She had started to feel furious, which she took as a good sign. She couldn't believe the town council had let Ms Oleander buy the boardwalk. She couldn't believe more people hadn't signed the petition. She couldn't believe they hadn't found the treasure. She couldn't believe she was in bed sick while her friends were preparing a last-ditch attempt to save them all. She aimed a vicious kick at her desk, knocking her shelf and sending a number of things raining down on her head. This did nothing to improve her mood.

She rubbed the sore spot on her head, then scooped up the fallen items and dumped them in a pile on her desk. She'd sort them out later, when she didn't feel so rubbish. She picked her puzzle box up out of the pile and flopped back on the bed, twisting its pieces into new and interesting configurations. At least her own treasures were safe in here, out of reach of Ms Oleander.

She sat bolt upright, her hands tightening on the box. She used the puzzle box to keep her treasures safe. What was to say that the pirates hadn't done something similar? Her mind raced. Maybe they had missed something in the cave. They'd been looking for treasure. But maybe they should have been looking for a puzzle. She wracked her brains, trying to call up images of the inside of the cave. But she hadn't been paying enough attention. She'd been looking for something big and flashy. If the pirates had wanted their treasure to stay buried, she should have been looking for something properly hidden.

She stood up, testing her balance. A few fuzzy spots danced round the edges of her vision but nothing too dramatic. She felt better than she had in days. She pulled on some jeans, shoved a hoody on over her pyjama top, stuck the puzzle box in her pocket and tore down the hall to Teddy's room. She knocked quietly on the door. There was no answer.

"Teddy!" she hissed. "It's me, open up."

"Go away," came Teddy's muffled voice. It sounded like he might have his head under the covers.

"No, I'm serious, open the door. I think I have an idea." No response again. "Don't make me go and get the master key."

There was an earth-moving sigh, followed by the creak of bedsprings and the sound of someone dragging their feet across the carpet. The door opened just a little.

"What do you want?" said Teddy.

Freya planted two hands on his chest and shoved him back into the room. She stepped inside and closed the door in one swift movement.

He rounded on her furiously, but she held out her palms.

"I know, I know. You hate me. You never want to

speak to me again despite living in my B&B. I get it. Just give me two minutes." She pulled the puzzle box out of her pocket and tossed it to him.

"What's this supposed to be?" he said, holding it up and squinting at it.

"Open it and see," she said.

Teddy rolled his eyes and gave the lid a sharp tug. Nothing happened. He frowned and brought the box up to his eyeline. He dug his fingers round the edge of the lid, bracing the box between his knees and pulling.

"It's stuck," he said, throwing it back to her. "Is that it? You got it stuck and wanted me to open it for you?"

"It's not stuck," said Freya, rotating the pieces of the box. "It's locked."

She pushed a button and the box sprang open.

Teddy's eyebrows flew up. He took the box back from her and swung the lid back and forth on its hinge. "Neat trick," he said with a shrug. "And I care about this because…?"

"Because what if we missed something back in the

cave? Something like this."

Teddy sat down on the bed, turning the box over in his hands. "You think the pirates built something to hide their treasure in? As if burying it in a cave wasn't protection enough?"

Freya sat down beside him. "It wouldn't have been, though, not back then. Edge was a smuggler's paradise back in the day. There are tunnels and stuff all over town. The caves would have been getting a whole lot more traffic back then than they do now."

Teddy considered this. "It's possible."

"It is possible. And that makes it worth a look." Freya was practically bouncing on the bed. "Come on, we know our way now and everything. We could be in and out before dinner time."

Teddy clicked the box closed and tried to open it again. It wouldn't open. He scowled. "Show me how this works," he said.

"No," said Freya smugly. "That's the whole point. I'm the only one who knows how to open it."

He gave it another stubborn tug and then when it didn't open put it down on the bed between them.

Freya popped it open, relishing the look of fury on Teddy's face.

"So what makes you think you'll be able to open a pirate's version? If only one person is supposed to know how to open it?"

Freya grinned. "This is kind of my whole thing. If we find it, I'll be able to open it."

Freya wished she felt half as confident as she sounded. But she knew Teddy wouldn't move for a maybe. Not finding the treasure the first time had broken his heart. She waited, holding her breath.

Eventually he sighed. "OK, fine. I suppose it's worth a look."

"Yes!" she cheered, grabbing him in an awkward grip halfway between a hug and a headlock.

He shoved her off roughly, turning pink round the ears and trying very hard not to look pleased.

Freya looked at her watch. "Hey, we'd better get moving if we want to catch Lin before she heads to the protest."

"OK then, let's get out of here."

* * *

Lin was not as happy to see them as Freya had hoped she might be.

She was holding a glue gun, which she pointed at Teddy. "I thought you never wanted to speak to me ever, ever, ever again. And you –" she pointed the glue gun at Freya – "are supposed to be in bed, too sick to come over and help make banners or calm Mei down."

Freya grinned. "When has my presence ever helped calm Mei down?"

Lin rolled her eyes. "Well, better late than never, I suppose. Come on in."

"Lin," started Freya, but Lin was already halfway down the hall.

"We can just tell my mum that Teddy is from the city, which is technically true," Lin called back over her shoulder. "There's a bunch of Mei's friends bussing in to support us, so I don't think she'll ask any questions."

"Lin!" yelled Freya. "Would you stop talking for five seconds? We're not coming in. You have to come with us."

Lin scoffed and folded her arms. "This is going to be

good. Where are we going now? One hour before my sister's big protest to save your boardwalk, I might add."

Freya quickly explained. Lin pursed her lips and leaned against the wall.

"It's got to be worth a look," added Freya, half sure that Lin was only pretending to hesitate.

Lin sighed and put the glue gun down on the table. "You know Mei is going to murder me, right? If my mum doesn't get there first."

"Only if we're wrong," said Freya with a grin. "Besides, hopefully the crowds will be big enough that she won't even notice you're not there."

"Quite possibly. She does seem to have roped in every single person she's ever met. And they're all in my kitchen."

There was a sudden crash and a yelp from the kitchen. Lin jumped about half a metre in the air. She started shoving her feet into her boots. "Right, it sounds like things are getting violent in there. Let's go before someone spots you and forces you to paint something."

A few minutes later, they made their way along the promenade, dropping to the sand with a series of wet thwacks. They were sure-footed this time. Freya felt as though she could dance her way to the cave. Or at least, she did until a furious attack of coughing bent her double. She leaned back against a rock, wheezing gently.

Lin raised her eyebrows. "Are you sure you're up for this?"

Freya waved her away. "Doesn't matter. The sale goes through this evening. It has to be today."

They retraced their footsteps, following their memories, Teddy's map and the occasional smudge of yellow chalk. Freya couldn't believe her eyes when they squeezed through the tunnel and found themselves standing on the big yellow "X" that she'd drawn. The first time they'd come through, it felt like it had taken them hours. This time she couldn't believe how fast they'd gone, even with her stopping to cough every four seconds.

"OK," said Lin, switching the torch nervously between her hands, "what's the plan?"

"Same as last time," said Freya. "We still have to search each of the caves. But this time we're looking for something small. Something that blends in with the rest of the cave but that shouldn't be there."

"So we're trying to spot something that's been specifically designed not to be spotted?" asked Teddy.

"Exactly," said Freya, planting her left palm on the wall of the cave. "So concentrate."

Freya's nerves rose to a feverish pitch as they made their way into the first cave. Or maybe it was her actual fever. Either way, her hands were shaking as they patted the wall. Lin swept the torch in front of them in regimented stripes, starting at their feet and working her way up the wall. Freya swept the wall with the metal detector. Last time, they'd concentrated on the ground, thinking they were looking for something buried under their feet, rather than hidden under their fingertips. They had no luck in the first cave. They couldn't find anything that didn't look like it belonged there.

Freya tried to ignore the sinking feeling in her chest as they moved to the second cave. The air was thick with the smell of seaweed and rancid water and something else rotten. If this plan didn't work, this was it. She'd felt like this before but this was really, really it. If they didn't find something today, the sale would go through and Ms Oleander would be free to tear up the boardwalk. They felt their way round the walls, not speaking. Freya moved the metal detector in large, slow circles. When it gave a screech, she got such a fright that she almost dropped it. Lin and Teddy were by her side in seconds.

Under the light of Lin's torch, Freya moved the detector across the wall in smaller and smaller rings until she had pinpointed the area that was pinging its alarm. She pulled the chalk from her pocket with one hand and drew a circle round it. Then she handed the metal detector back to Lin, took the torch and started examining the rock more closely. At first, her fingers found only more rough rock. Then her hand moved over something cold and thin. At first she had taken it for a rivulet of water, but this time she stopped, running her thumb over it more slowly. She angled the torch so it was shining upwards and the light glinted off something tiny in the cave wall. She pushed her glasses up her nose and bent to look closely, the tip of her nose almost touching the rock.

There, embedded in the wall, was a tiny metal tube.

Twenty

"What is it?" said Teddy impatiently, craning to look.

Freya elbowed him in the ribs. "You're blocking the light. Stand back."

Teddy slouched back huffily, jamming his hands into his pockets.

Lin rocked back and forth on the balls of her feet. "Seriously, though," she said, "what is it?"

"I'm not sure yet," murmured Freya, running the pad of her thumb along the length of the tube, "but it's something. Something that's not like everything else."

She lifted the torch and shone it down. The light picked out tiny grooves running across the face of the tube.

"Oh," said Freya. "*Oh.* I think it's a hinge." A grin split her face. "And if there's a hinge, there's a moving part."

She grabbed the chalk again and started to shade in a line from the top to the bottom of the hinge. There was a tiny hairline crack in the rock face. Freya followed it with the chalk until there was a square about the size of her hand outlined in the wall. She stepped back, wiping her fingers on her trousers, leaving cloudy yellow smudges down her legs.

"What's that?" asked Teddy.

Freya rolled her eyes. "I don't know yet. Give me a sec."

She found the hinge with her thumb again and traced the fingers of her other hand down the opposite side of the square. She dug her fingernails into the tiny gap and pulled hard. Ever so slowly, a millimetre at a time, the square started to swing open.

"Whoa," said Teddy.

"What he said," said Lin.

With a sickening crunch the square loosened and slammed back on its hinge, exposing the space underneath.

There was nothing there.

Freya frowned and shone the torch around the space. Nothing. It was just a square hole carved into the rock. She swung the rocky flap closed again and it slotted perfectly into place, almost invisible. She rubbed a hand across her forehead and pulled the square back out. "It doesn't make any sense," she said. "Why would someone carve out this space and then not put anything in it?"

"It's too small to hide treasure in," said Lin, stepping beside Freya and peering in.

"It's too small to hide anything in," said Freya, tracing the flap with her fingertips.

"So what's the point?" asked Lin.

"What is the point?" echoed Freya, although she wasn't really talking to anyone. She pulled her hair back into a messy ponytail and stood back to look at the wall.

"Do you hear that?" asked Teddy.

Freya cocked her head. "Hear what?"

Teddy held up a hand. "Shh. Wait a second."

Freya listened. All of a sudden she could hear it. A shifting, rumbling, crunching sound coming from deep within the rocks.

"It's a cave-in!" yelled Lin. "Run!"

"Wait!" shouted Freya, before Lin could bounce away with the light. "I don't think it is."

Lin stopped and turned. Freya's mouth dropped open as, with a horrendous grinding sound, part of the cave began to move. A long narrow piece of rock slid down into the gap created by the hinged flap.

"Oh," said Freya. "Oh!"

"Stop saying 'oh' and say something else," said Lin.

Freya took the torch from her and took a few steps back. "Oh, wow," she said.

"What is it?" hissed Teddy. "What's happening?"

Freya's pulse was thumping in her throat. It was like one of those optical illusion pictures that looks like random lines or squiggles, and it's only when you look a certain way that you realise there's a picture in there. Now that she could see the seams where the piece of rock had shifted, the rest of the wall clicked into place in her mind. Lines she'd barely looked at, which she'd assumed were cracks or waterdrops or patterns in the rock, suddenly stood out as brightly as if she'd drawn them with her yellow chalk.

"This is it," she said. "This is their puzzle box."

"How do you know?" said Lin, squinting up at the rock. "I don't think I'm seeing whatever you're seeing."

"Yeah," said Teddy. "What are we meant to be looking at?"

"It's a puzzle," said Freya, "like those old ones you'd get in Christmas crackers."

She stood on her tiptoes, stretching up to where the new gap in the wall had appeared. She planted her palms beside it and shoved. Nothing happened. She swore under her breath, gritted her teeth and threw her whole weight against it. It moved just a little. But it was enough to see a gap start to open on the other side.

"None of these gaps are big enough to get through, though," said Teddy. "Or to put anything inside."

"Yeah," said Lin. "I guess you could feed your treasure through the hole but how on earth would you get it back out?"

"I don't think the moving parts are the door," said Freya. "I think they're the key."

She stood back, letting the torch play over the wall, astonished at what she was seeing.

Lin sighed impatiently and shunted her in the back. "Say more things. Like a Christmas cracker puzzle?"

"Yes! The little sliding-tile puzzles. Look, the wall is made up of all these different pieces, all different shapes and sizes. I don't think they pull out of the wall." She wrapped her fingers underneath one of the pieces, planted a foot against the wall and yanked until her knuckles felt like they might pop. "No, they definitely don't come out of the wall. But they slide."

She pushed against the piece of wall that had moved. It slid more easily now, clicking against the frame on the other side. She stood back and brushed the dust from her palms. "I think there is some kind of order these pieces need to be arranged in. And if we can get them there, the door will unlock."

Lin pursed her lips and nodded. "OK, so how do we know what shape they're supposed to be in?"

Freya traced the edge of the shapes with one hand. "It's an irregular shape. See all the bits jutting out? I bet if you arranged them into a rectangle, it would open. That's how keys normally work. They push a load of jagged bits into a straight line."

"If you think the treasure is behind here, could we not just bash it open?" asked Teddy.

"Sure," said Freya. "In fact, I imagine that's exactly Ms Oleander's plan. I can't see her messing about with puzzles and locks. So if you can get your hands on a battering ram or a great big drill before tomorrow, we're laughing."

"OK," said Teddy slowly, "point taken. So how do you get the pieces into a rectangle?"

Freya rolled her eyes and tightened her ponytail. "That's the puzzle bit."

"And how do we puzzle it out?" asked Teddy.

Freya turned to him with a raised eyebrow. "You give me a bit of quiet, that's how."

She stared at the wall until the shapes were imprinted on her mind. Then she sat down on the floor of the cave, rested her head in her hands and thought hard. She moved the pieces in her mind, imagining all the ways they could sit, pointedly ignoring her friends fidgeting behind her.

"OK," she said finally, taking the chalk back out of her pocket. "I think this is our final shape."

She sketched it on the ground, numbering each piece. Then she turned and scribbled the numbers on to the puzzle pieces in the wall.

"So I think the first thing we need to do is to get this piece –" she pointed – "over here."

"Oh," said Lin, smiling. "I've been training my whole life for this."

Freya turned to her. "What do you mean?"

"Figuring out how to get a tile from one place to another? What does that sound like to you?"

Freya frowned and then laughed. The sound

ricocheted around the cave.

"I'm lost again," said Teddy. "What does it sound like?"

"It sounds like a Rubik's Cube," said Freya.

As Freya explained where each piece had to go, Lin puzzled out how to get it there. The three of them pushed and tugged and heaved the pieces in front of them. As they went, Freya's brain started to get the hang of it. This was her favourite thing about working on a new puzzle or taking apart a new machine. After a while, the pattern would emerge. It felt like something invisible suddenly dancing up and flicking you in the nose. She felt fairly sure that she'd be able to do Rubik's Cube now. She bit down on her lip as the final piece clicked into place. The yellow shape in front of them was now a perfect rectangle.

"Here goes nothing," she said.

She braced one shoulder against the wall and started to shove. Sweat beaded on the back of her neck, making her shiver. The other two fell in on either side of her, heaving all their weight against the wall. A groaning, creaking sound rose around them.

"It's moving!" yelled Teddy. "I can't believe it; it's really moving!"

Ever so slowly the cave wall in front of them moved away, revealing a long, dark passageway. The temperature seemed to drop again, the black tunnel radiating cold.

Teddy exclaimed and went to move.

Lin put an arm in front of him. "Excuse me, what happened to ladies first?" She tossed the torch back to Freya.

Freya caught it in her right hand, stretching her left behind her to take Lin's hand. Lin reached her hand out to take Teddy's. He let her and slowly the three of them made their way into the dark.

Twenty-One

The only sound was the shuffling of their footsteps and their shivery breath. Even the dripping water hadn't made it this far into the cave. The tunnel turned sharply and Freya bashed into the wall in front of her. She seethed, examining her skinned knuckles. They looked red and angry but weren't bleeding. And most importantly the torch had survived. She swivelled its beam down the twist of the tunnel.

"I see something," she hissed.

"Does it look like a great big treasure chest?" whispered Lin.

Freya didn't answer. There was a vague shape about halfway up one of the walls but she couldn't make it out in the murk.

"Oh!" she yelled, as she got close. "Check this out!" She reached upwards and pulled down an old torch. She passed it back to Lin.

"This must be how they found their way around without batteries," said Lin. She swept the torch in a dramatic arc. "It's like something out of an old movie. All we're missing are the massive spiderwebs."

Teddy shuddered. "I don't like spiders."

"Me neither," said Freya.

"Babies," said Lin. "Spiders are your friends. Anyway, I think you're safe. Not even the spiders have made it down here. It's a shame we don't have anything to light it with."

"We already have a torch," said Freya.

"I know," said Lin. "This just feels more appropriate."

Teddy cleared his throat, pulled a lighter from his pocket and lit it with a click.

"What on earth are you doing with a lighter?" said Freya.

Teddy rolled his eyes. "I had to build fires in my cave, remember?"

Freya put her hands on her hips but Lin just dipped the torch towards the flame with a grin. It whooshed into life, throwing flickering orange light around the narrow tunnel.

"Oh yes, now we're talking," said Lin, brandishing the flaming torch like a sword.

"Would you be careful?" said Freya, leaping out of the way.

Lin cackled and did not get any more careful.

"This means there's really something here," said Teddy quietly. "We really might find the treasure."

That caught Lin's attention. They stood in a circle looking at each other, the torch flickering between them.

"For goodness' sake," said Freya, "let's go. We can't just stand here staring at each other until Ms Oleander bashes through the ceiling in a digger."

She took the battery torch from Lin, who was having more fun with the fire torch anyway, and began to move ahead. She hadn't walked more than a few metres when her toes collided with something, almost sending her sprawling. She stepped back and swept her light downwards. She'd tripped on a metal ring of torches lying on the ground; a long rope attached them to the roof. Lin lit them with a quick swoop of her flame and Teddy wrapped the rope round his arm, hoisting the makeshift chandelier upwards. He tied it in place with a winding knot. The tunnel had opened up into another cave, smaller than the ones they'd previously passed through.

"Oh," said Freya, blinking in the wash of light.

Every surface glittered. Platters of burnished golden coins, glowing amber in the firelight. Ropes of pearls. Jewels winking like raindrops. An enormous wooden chest, straight out of the cartoons, was placed in the middle of the room.

The three of them stood there in absolute silence. Freya took off her glasses and rubbed her eyes. She had a sudden horrible thought that maybe all this was some kind of feverish delusion, that she was tucked up in bed in the B&B dreaming the whole thing. She looked around. She didn't think so. She started to laugh. Once she'd started, she found she couldn't stop and she doubled over, hands braced against her knees. She laughed until her stomach hurt, until her throat felt scraped, until tears rolled down her face, but she couldn't stop. Lin hit the ground beside her, laughing just as hard. Even Teddy was laughing, his face bright with it, tears gathering in his eyes.

Freya sat down beside Lin. She reached out and pushed her hand through a pile of coins, relishing the surreal feeling of slippery gold across her skin. She ran her fingers through a rail of pearl necklaces above her, sending them swaying. The world's most expensive wind chime. Teddy, the only one still on his feet, made a dash for the chest in the middle of the room. His face triumphant, he seized the lid and threw it open.

"Wait!" shouted Lin, throwing up a hand.

She was too late. The thin wire she'd spotted snapped, slicing viciously at Teddy's cheek as it flew upwards. He let go of the lid with a cry, one hand flying to his face. The door behind them slammed shut, extinguishing the flames while the other torch skittered across the ground, plunging them into complete darkness. There was a moment of quiet as the cave settled itself around them.

Freya patted around for the torch, her heart hammering against her ribs. Her fingers closed round it and she switched it on, her shaking hands sending the light bouncing wildly around the cave.

"Is everyone OK?" she shouted, swinging the torch around to try to find her friends.

Dust from the moving rocks coated her tongue as she opened her mouth and she coughed. She scrubbed her tongue with the back of one hand but her hands were just as dusty.

"I'm fine," said Lin, coming from behind Freya and touching her arm. "Teddy?"

"I'm all right," came Teddy's voice, although it sounded thick.

Freya pointed the torch towards him, the beam picking him out by the chest. He had one hand clamped to his cheek. The blood pumping between his fingers looked black and sticky in the gloom.

"Oh," said Freya, running towards him, her feet

sliding on the shifting coins covering the ground. "Teddy, you're hurt."

"It's all right," he said, although speaking made him wince. "I'm pretty sure it looks worse than it is."

"It looks pretty bad," said Lin.

"It's just a cut," said Teddy, prodding at the inside of his cheek with his tongue. "It didn't go all the way through."

Picturing Teddy's tongue poking through a hole in his cheek made Freya feel faint and she had to dig her fingernails into her palm to stay upright. She leaned back against the chest and took a few deep breaths.

"Here," said Lin, gesturing for the torch.

She walked a quick circle round the chest. "I don't see anything else," she said.

She took hold of the lid and gingerly eased it open. She pointed the torch inside, her mouth set in a grim line.

"It's empty," she said. "It's just a booby trap."

"Stupid," said Teddy. "I shouldn't have touched it."

Freya reached out and touched his arm. "Don't be daft. How could you have realised?"

"She did," he said, gesturing at Lin.

"That's because my eyes are never where they're supposed to be," said Lin. "Really, don't worry about it."

"Any one of us could have opened it," said Freya.

Teddy shook his head. "Never mind that. How do we get out?"

Twenty-Two

Freya pointed the torch around until they located the rope holding the chandelier. Teddy untied his knot, let down the circle of torches and lit them again with his lighter.

"Let there be light," he murmured, as he hoisted the chandelier back into place.

The orangey glow of flames glinting on gold stole Freya's breath from her lungs again. She ran in quick, light steps back down the tunnel they'd come through. The rock face had closed up and stared impassively down at her.

"No puzzle on this side," she said, running a flat palm over the surface. "And nothing to grip on to, to pull it back open."

A finger of cold slid down her spine. They were stuck. She felt the familiar panic starting to rise.

Teddy stubbornly stuck his fingers into the gap and gave it a tug. Nothing happened. "Maybe we could use the rope from the chandelier," he said. His voice sounded tight. "Tie it round something and pull?"

"Maybe," said Freya quietly, outlining the door with her torch.

"What are you thinking?" said Lin, squeezing in beside her.

"I'm not sure. Something is bugging me."

"What?"

"I don't know. Give me a second."

She wandered back along the tunnel to the treasure room. Her heart felt as though it was stuck in her throat. She couldn't think around the panic that they'd be stuck in this cave forever. But there was something. Something just on the edge of her mind. She took a slow, deep breath. She tried to picture her terror as a solid lump. Slowly, panel by panel, she built a box round it and pushed it out of the way. She took down her ponytail, shaking it out and rubbing her head before scooping it back into place again. The thought at the back of her mind surfaced.

"What if you set off your own booby trap?" she asked.

Teddy emerged from the passage. "That'd be pretty daft."

"True," said Freya, "but people do daft stuff all the time. I've done about eighteen different daft things today."

Teddy shrugged. "I guess then you'd be stuck."

Freya shook her head. "I don't think so. I think there must be another way out. That's what I would do."

"An emergency exit?" said Lin.

"Exactly. There's always a way out."

The thought opened up a chink of light in the darkness of Freya's fear and she felt her shoulders loosen just a little. She started to make a slow circuit of the room, looking for anything unusual. Well, more unusual than everything else. On one side she came upon a beautiful wooden wheel, like the wheel you'd use to steer a ship. She wrapped her hands round the spokes, the smooth wood soothing under her palms. She gave it a sharp tug. It was stuck fast. She tried again. No luck. But as she pressed against the wheel, she could hear a gravelly crunching sound. It sounded like the door they'd come through. But it was coming from the wrong direction. Somewhere there was another moving part.

"Hey!" she shouted. "Can you two look around and see if anything looks like it's trying to move?"

Freya wedged a shoulder under one of the spokes on the wheel and pushed her weight against it. The silvery sound of falling coins floated through the air.

"Here!" shouted Lin, waving. "There are coins sliding about over here!"

Freya gave the wheel another heave. Another tinkling shower of coins. Freya let go of the wheel and ran to where her friends were crouched. They got on their knees and started to scoop out handfuls of coins, digging up whatever the wheel was trying to move. Freya's fingers brushed something thick and rough. She grabbed hold and gave it an almighty yank. She had found an enormous piece of rope, almost the thickness of her arm.

"What the—" said Teddy, shuffling around beside her.

"No idea," said Freya, sliding both hands underneath the rope, then standing up and pulling.

Her feet scrabbled for purchase on the slippery ground and she saw a ripple of movement snaking through the coins carpeting the floor. They followed the length of rope until they had almost reached the wall, where a massive tug brought it free, spraying coins everywhere.

"Ouch!" she yelled, as they rained down on her and her friends.

"That looks a lot more fun in the movies," said Teddy, rubbing his head.

The rope ran up the wall and back down again. Freya followed it back towards the wheel she'd been turning. She tipped her head back, trying to see the roof.

"It's some kind of pulley," she said, pointing. "The

rope must be looped round something up there. One end is attached to the wheel."

She took hold of the wheel again and pushed. It still didn't move much, but freed of the weight of the coins the rope tautened, creating a sharp triangle pointing towards the ceiling.

"OK," said Lin, "and the other end?"

Freya's heart started to hammer again but this time it was with excitement.

"It must be attached to a door."

They followed the rope back to where it disappeared under the carpet of coins. They fell back on their knees, shovelling piles of gold. Freya sat down and used her feet like wipers, shoving rippling stacks of coins away from her.

"Here!" she shouted, as her feet collided with something hard.

They scrabbled at the coins, unearthing a huge metal ring that was plugged into the floor. They started to clear the surrounding space. Freya squealed as the outline of a square came into view.

"Look!" she said. "The wheel is trying to lift this

piece of the floor. The way out must be through here."

Lin squinted at it. "I would have expected us to be going up to get out, not further down."

"Yeah," said Freya, "that's true. This must be it, though. How many secret entrances can one room have?"

"At least two apparently," said Teddy with a grin that looked more like a grimace.

The three of them were getting giggly with nerves.

Freya forced herself to take another long, deep breath. "All right," she said. "We probably need two of us to turn the wheel, and one person to stay here and see what's underneath this piece of floor."

Lin hauled herself to her feet. "You've already had a go at turning the wheel. Why don't you give Teddy and me a shot?"

Freya stretched her arms. They did feel a bit achy. She nodded. "OK. Turn anticlockwise."

Lin gave a salute and helped Teddy to his feet. They moved over to the wheel. Freya gave a thumbs up and rolled on to her stomach beside the trapdoor, her face propped in her hands. Teddy and Lin started to pull, heaving their body weight against the wheel. With a groan the square in front of Freya began to move.

"Almost there!" she called over.

The only answer was a series of grunts. The slab started to lift towards the ceiling. Freya ducked out of the way as a corner began to drift towards her. She stared at the space where the slab had been sitting. There was nothing there. She blinked at it. The terror she'd managed to push away came crashing back. She put a hand to her chest. It felt hard to breathe.

"What's going on over there?" asked Lin.

"I don't know," said Freya.

"Well, could you hurry up and figure it out?" yelled Teddy.

Freya swept her arm quickly underneath the dangling slab, feeling for any hidden crevice she might have missed.

"There's nothing here," she shouted.

"What? Maybe you should come lift and one of us can take a look," shouted Teddy.

"I'm telling you, there's nothing here."

The slab fell back to the ground with a crunch.

"I don't get it," said Lin. "If there's nothing under there, why rig up this whole big system to lift it?"

Freya scuffed at the ground with her toe. There had to be something she wasn't seeing. More to the puzzle. She stood back and looked again at the rope.

"Wait," she said, "maybe Lin was right."

"I usually am," said Lin. "Right about what?"

"Maybe the way out isn't to go further down," she said, craning her neck to peer into the gloom at the roof of the cave. "Maybe it's to go up."

Twenty-Three

"It's the only thing that makes sense," said Freya. "If the answer isn't underneath the slab, it has to be up there." She pointed towards the roof.

Lin nodded slowly. "So one of us has to go up there and check it out."

"I think so," replied Freya. "Which of us is the smallest?"

"Teddy," said Lin, completely straight-faced.

He scowled. "I am *not*."

Lin winked at Freya over his shoulder.

"It's definitely me, isn't it?" asked Freya.

"Are you just saying that so you don't have to do the heavy lifting?" said Lin, a grin in the corner of her mouth.

Freya fixed her with a look. "You know I'd rather be down here than up there."

She had never been all that great with heights. This month was starting to feel like a cruel joke. If they did find a door, it would probably lead to a clown convention or a spider-petting zoo.

She pinched the bridge of her nose. "OK," she said. "I'll climb on, you two hoist me up and I can see whatever is going on up there."

"How do we know you won't just leave us if you find a door up there?" asked Teddy.

"Abject betrayal isn't really Freya's style," said Lin, "although it's a good question."

"Thanks a bunch," said Freya.

"Not whether you would leave us," said Lin, "but if someone has to turn the wheel and the other person gets hoisted up to some kind of door, how does the person turning the wheel get out?"

"I have no idea. Hopefully not by me running the

long way round and opening the puzzle door. That would be very annoying."

"Less annoying than starving to death in a treasure cave, though."

"True. Let me get up there and see what we're dealing with. Then we can make a plan."

Freya sat down on the middle of the slab, wrapping her arms and legs round the rope at its middle. Teddy and Lin returned to the wheel.

"OK, we're going to start turning," yelled Lin. "Are you ready?"

Freya tightened her grip. Her throat felt like sandpaper. She swallowed. "Ready!"

Teddy and Lin reached up over the side of the wheel and started dragging the spokes downwards. Freya gave a squeal as she started to lift into the air. She was as close to the middle of the slab as she could manage but it still wobbled as it moved. She tried very hard not to picture herself sliding off one end and landing with a splat among all the gold coins. The harder she tried, the harder she pictured it.

The cave looked even more incredible as she

climbed higher, the glimmer of the treasure glowing against the dark walls like a candle in a lantern. After a while, as Teddy and Lin grew smaller, looking down started to make her feel dizzy. She tore her eyes from the gilded floor and forced herself to look at the walls.

"Stop!" she shouted, as a strange-looking object came into view. "Hold it there!"

The slab came to a shaky halt, shuddering in the air as Teddy and Lin struggled to keep the wheel still. Freya reluctantly unwound one hand from the rope and felt in her pocket for the torch. She clicked it on and pointed it into the murk. Close to the wall was a hook. The hook was attached to another rope. Freya frowned, following the line of the second rope with her torch. Her eyes blazed as she suddenly understood.

"Oh!" she yelled. "*Oh*."

"Oh what?" Lin yelled back.

"No, don't worry about it," groaned Teddy. "Take your time. Really savour the moment."

His sarcasm didn't even touch Freya. Her mouth

was dangling open as her mind clicked together the different pieces of the mechanism. There was a way out. There always was. And she had found it.

"It's genius!" she called.

"Can it be genius a little faster?" shouted Lin. "My knuckles feel like they're about to pop."

Freya stretched her free hand out towards the hook but she couldn't reach. It had been designed for an adult and she was way too short. The slab wobbled underneath her as Teddy and Lin strained to hold it. She sucked in a deep breath through clenched teeth. She wrapped her legs tighter round the rope, locking her ankles round each other. Then, without giving herself a chance to think too hard about it, she started to lie back on the slab.

"Freya!" yelled Lin. "Stop it! What are you doing?"

"Just hold it steady!" she shouted back.

Sweat pricked her back, slicking her T-shirt against her skin. Her teeth were chattering and she clamped them together to shut them up. As she lay back, she let go of the rope with both hands, stretching fully towards the hook. The slab tipped as her weight shifted and Freya felt the rope dig into the backs of her knees. She found herself looking straight at the ground. She couldn't help it. She screamed. The slab dropped a few metres as Lin's hands loosened on the wheel. Freya let out a whimper and closed her eyes. She didn't want the ground to rush up to meet her.

The rope bit savagely into her legs as the slab came to a sudden stop. Freya didn't dare open her eyes. She felt herself move tentatively upwards and after a few seconds she peeled open one eyelid. She was still looking down at the ground, Lin and Teddy's pasty faces staring back up at her. She tipped her own face back towards the ceiling, pressing one hand to her glasses, which had slid perilously close to the top of her head. She was back in line with the hook. She stretched herself out to her full length and reached for it again. Her fingertips just brushed it. She yelled in frustration. Her stomach boiled, the muscles in her back screaming. Sending up a silent prayer, she loosened her legs just a little. This time she closed her fingers round the hook and, with a roar of triumph, used her legs to pull herself back to the centre of the platform.

She just sat there for a moment, her arms wrapped round the rope in the centre, her hand like a claw round the hook. Her whole body was shaking. The swaying of the platform reminded her that her friends were struggling to hold the wheel underneath her. She shook herself and clamped the hook round the ring in the middle of the platform.

"OK," she shouted down to them, "let go."

"Have you lost your mind?" yelled Lin. "We're not letting go!"

"I promise it's safe," shouted Freya. "It's genius. Let go and you'll see!"

Freya leaned back, not letting go of the rope this time, and peered down at her friends. Teddy gave her a nod and stepped away from the wheel. Lin groaned under the increased load. She did not look happy. But after a few seconds she reluctantly did the same.

The slab dropped. Only a little but it was enough to have Freya regretting every single decision that had led to this moment. When it stopped, her screams were reverberating around the cave. She gathered herself, trying to calm her racing heart. She moved her arms out of the way and looked at the hook. As she'd hoped, the rope at the end of the hook had tautened and was now holding the weight of the slab. She frowned.

"What now?" shouted Teddy. "Can you see a door up there?"

Freya shook her head. "That's not how it works."

"How what works?"

Freya sighed. She'd been hoping to just show them. Much cooler that way.

"It's like the lighthouse," she yelled.

"Are you having some kind of break with reality?" shouted Lin. "What are you talking about?"

Freya leaned over the edge of the slab so she could see them. "It's like how the lighthouse turns. Remember, they showed us?"

"Why don't you pretend I wasn't paying attention and explain it to me again?" said Lin.

Freya laughed. "The lighthouse works like a big wind-up toy. You turn a wheel that lifts a weight in the middle of the tower and then as it drops, the weight turns the lamp."

"OK?" said Lin.

"So I think this is the same," said Freya. "The wheel is … well, the wheel. It lifts up the slab as its weight. Then you hook the slab on to whatever this is, and as the slab drops I reckon it's going to pull open a door."

"Oh, that is pretty genius," said Lin. "Are you sure they told us about that when we visited the lighthouse?"

"Yes, I am. You were probably watching a seagull fight a tourist or something."

Lin sighed wistfully. "I do love watching seagulls fight tourists."

"Yes, yes, it's all very impressive," said Teddy impatiently, "except that we've got one big problem."

"The slab isn't dropping," said Freya.

"The slab isn't dropping," echoed Teddy.

"It was obviously made for an adult. I'm not heavy enough."

"She felt plenty heavy enough," said Teddy, rubbing his arms.

"So we make you heavier," said Lin.

"And how do we do that?" asked Freya.

Lin scuffed her shoe along the ground, sending a spill of coins flying. "We load you up."

Grinning, Freya pulled her backpack from her back and took out the length of slim rope inside. She knotted it round the handle of her bag, looped the other end through the ring on the slab and lowered it down to the others.

"Just dump everything out," she yelled. "We can deal with that later."

"Totally," called Lin. "Who wouldn't rather have diamonds than schoolbooks?"

Lin and Teddy gigglingly collected armfuls of treasure, shoving them into Freya's backpack. They didn't stop to look at what they were throwing in, just packed it as full as they could. After a few minutes, Lin tugged twice on the rope and Freya started to hoist the bag up. The slab tilted drunkenly under her as she shifted her centre of balance but she barely noticed. She hauled the backpack on to the platform and planted it between her legs. The slab didn't move. She upended the bag, sparkling treasures spilling out all around her. Then she tossed the bag over the side of the slab and started to let it down again.

"Not enough!" she called. "I demand more riches!"

As Teddy and Lin scooted around below her filling the bag, Freya arranged the treasures around her. She stuffed her pockets with gold coins and loose gemstones in every imaginable colour. She wrapped ropes of pearls round her neck, stacked so many rings on each finger that it became hard to close her fist. Every time the bag came up, her loot grew.

"I feel like a dragon!" she yelled down to her friends.

"When we get out of here, you can eat Ms Oleander," called Teddy.

She cried out as the slab gave a shudder under her. She bounced up and down, trying to make herself as heavy as possible. The slab groaned as it shifted a few centimetres and then stopped stubbornly again.

"One more load," shouted Freya, "and I think it'll go."

Another bag was hoisted up to her. Freya pulled it towards her and set it down between her legs. She didn't even have time to tip it out before the slab started to drop.

"It's working!" she shrieked.

She strained her ears, listening for a corresponding sound somewhere in the cave. Sure enough, a groaning, grinding noise rose from deep within the walls. A section of wall had started to lift, dislodging a gleaming waterfall of jewels. The slab dropped back into its space on the ground with a crunch. Freya burst out laughing as she came level with her friends. They were as festooned as she was. Lin was holding a bejewelled staff. Teddy was wearing a tiara.

"It looks good on you," Freya said, tilting her head at him.

Teddy grinned. "Thanks. I always thought I'd make an excellent princess."

Freya made a move for the door but a shudder of the slab under her made her stop. *Focus*, she told herself. *You're not out of here yet.*

"We need to weigh down the platform so the door doesn't just close behind us. We need to find something me-sized or bigger," she said.

Lin and Teddy looked at each other, nodded and

ran in the same direction. They grabbed the wooden chest from the middle of the room and dragged it over, wheezing as they shoved it on to the slab. Lin sank down with her back against it and wiped her face with one sleeve. Teddy piled a few armfuls of treasure into the chest just to be safe and then stood back, shoving his hands in his pockets. Freya moved one foot off the slab, tentatively shifting her weight. When the slab didn't move, she stepped away completely. The rope groaned but the slab stayed where it was.

She planted her hands on her knees and started to laugh. Lin leaned her head back against the chest, grinning. Teddy grabbed Freya in a headlock and started to jump up and down. Freya shoved him off, cackling.

"OK," she said, struggling to catch her breath. "We've found the hidden treasure. We've escaped the death cave. What's next on the to-do list?"

"Isn't it obvious?" said Teddy, straightening his tiara and turning towards the door. "We stop the baddies."

Twenty-Four

The three followed the tunnel behind the secret door, climbing steadily upward.

"This path is a lot nicer than the other one," said Teddy.

"It is," said Freya. "We should lodge a complaint with the tourist board. We demand consistently accessible secret treasure trails."

The three of them were half hysterical, giggles bubbling barely beneath the surface. Without any warning at all, the tunnel spat them into a room. There were wooden floorboards under their feet, craggy unfinished walls and the most glorious thing Freya had ever seen: a small door.

"Bet that opens into another cave," said Lin.

"Don't even joke," said Freya, dashing towards it and throwing it open.

Sunlight streamed in, blinding them after so long in the gloom of the caves. Their accumulated jewels glittered, throwing rainbow specks around the room. Teddy and Lin piled through the door, dragging Freya with them. They had come through a small red door sitting innocently in one of Edge's whitewashed walls. There was a real house next door. Freya could see someone through the window doing the washing-up.

"This was here this whole time," murmured Freya.

"Although if you followed it from this end, you'd come up against a solid wall," said Lin. "Unless you already had someone on the other side ready to open it for you."

Teddy was blinking at the door like it was the weirdest thing he'd seen all day. "What is wrong with this town?"

Lin frowned. "What's that sound?"

Freya cocked her head. Lin was right. A rhythmic sound was floating down the streets towards them.

"Could it be the sea?" said Teddy. "It sometimes sounded so strange in the caves. Like voices or something."

"I think it is voices," said Freya.

Lin slapped a hand to her head. "Mei's protest! We must be close to the town hall."

Freya grabbed Lin by the arm and grinned. "You didn't miss it after all. Sister of the year!"

They dashed down the lane towards the sound, following the hum of voices through the maze of Edge's streets. As they drew closer, Freya could pick out individual voices and chants buzzing through a megaphone.

"We must be close," she yelled, throwing herself round another corner.

She stopped dead, the other two crashing into the back of her. Freya could see the march passing at the end of the road. But between it and them stood Ms Oleander. She was watching the protestors intently with a faint look of disgust.

Freya took Lin and Teddy by the wrists and started to quietly back away.

Ms Oleander glanced back towards them and did a cartoon double take.

"You," she said incredulously.

Freya frowned. The woman was living in her B&B, the least she could do was use her name. Then she realised Ms Oleander's jabbing finger was pointing past her, towards Teddy. She saw the wheels turning in Ms Oleander's brain as she took in the sight of the three of them together, filthy but bedecked in shimmering jewels. Her polite facade cracked and slipped away, her face curling into a scalding mask of fury.

"Nope," said Freya, turning and bolting away, the other two close at her heels.

They clattered round a corner, Ms Oleander's heels clacking furiously behind them. With her long scurrying legs and her footsteps snicking against the pavement, she reminded Freya of an insect more than ever. The kind that bit the head off its prey. She willed her feet to move faster.

"Towards the protest," she panted. "We can lose her in the crowd."

They scrambled down tiny twisting lanes, trying to follow the sound of chanting. Whatever Ms Oleander was planning, Freya was pretty sure she couldn't murder them in front of the entire town. Freya skidded to a stop as she glimpsed movement. She cried out in relief, dragging Teddy and Lin with her as she lurched towards the crowd. As they reached the end of the lane, Freya saw that they'd come out in front of the town hall. The street was crammed with protestors, colourful banners and signs swinging cheerily in the air.

"Whoa," said Lin. "Mei must be so happy."

Freya spotted Mei up at the front, standing on one of the town hall's plinths and yelling through a megaphone.

"Come on," she whispered. "We can blend into the crowd."

They started to make their way in, hoping the masses of people would swallow them up. That wasn't quite how it worked out. People fell silent as they passed, eyes wide as they took in the jewels winking out from the layers of grime. Freya gritted her teeth and instead started to make her way to the front. That way, they'd have the most witnesses.

Mei stopped yelling, sensing the disturbance. She craned her neck, frowning, trying to see what was going on Freya, Teddy and Lin stepped up on to the wide steps of the town hall. The square fell entirely silent; no one was really sure what they were looking at. There was a click and a flash from somewhere near the front of the crowd and when Freya turned towards it, she saw Sam the photographer staring at them, her mouth hanging open. She hadn't even bothered to raise her camera to her face, just pressed the button on instinct.

"Now what?" hissed Teddy through a clenched jaw.

Freya looked out into the sea of baffled faces. She took a deep breath. Blood. Heights. Caves. The dark. She reckoned she could face down one more fear. She marched over towards Mei, took the loudspeaker out of her hands and raised it in front of her face.

"Ms Oleander is a liar," she shouted. "She came to town with a proposal to buy the boardwalk for the town's own good. To develop it. To bring opportunities to Edge. To save us. But all she really wanted was to steal from us."

Freya dug her hand into one pocket and tossed a handful of gemstones into the crowd. They twinkled as they fell through the air, landing with a patter on the ground. There was a moment of dumbfounded silence and then people dropped to pick them up like birds falling on a scattering of breadcrumbs.

"We've just found these buried under the boardwalk. That's why she came to town. To dig our treasures right out from under us."

A gasp rippled through the crowd as Ms Oleander shoved her way towards them. She grabbed hold of Freya's wrist so hard that it hurt. Freya cried out and tried to wriggle away but Ms Oleander wrenched her back. Her knuckles were white round Freya's arm.

There was a commotion in the crowd and Freya looked up to see Granny Kate barrelling her way towards them. A figure closer to the front burst from the crowd, face ashen with fury under a bright hijab.

"Get your hands off her," said Ms Hanan. She didn't raise her voice but there was steel running through it all the same.

Freya shivered. Ms Hanan could be scary if she really wanted to.

Ms Oleander's lip curled but her grip on Freya loosened. She pushed her face close to Freya's. Freya flinched.

"Let me tell you right now, anything you found on my property is mine," she hissed.

"That's not true," said Teddy. "The law says—"

Ms Oleander cut him off with a stinging slap to the face. He fell backwards, his tiara flying off his head and skittering across the steps. Her hand was imprinted in scarlet on his cheek. Furious yells exploded from the crowd. In a blink there was a wall of bodies between the three of them and Ms Oleander. Ms Hanan threw herself at Ms Oleander with a screech and had to be hauled away by several other people.

Ms Oleander had lost all her carefully arranged

composure and was screaming now. "It's mine," she screeched. "You're too late."

"Actually they're not," came a voice from behind Freya.

The town council was standing on the steps. Catherine, the nice lady with the blonde bob, was looking at Ms Oleander in abject disgust. The mayor stood to one side, his forehead shiny, flapping his hands agitatedly. Catherine stepped round him. Ms Oleander belatedly tried to collect herself, tucking loose strands of hair behind her ears and smoothing down the front of her green coat. She took a step towards the council but Catherine raised a hand, stopping her in her tracks.

"All things considered," she said, her voice ringing against the cobbles, "I don't think that you have been negotiating with us in good faith."

The colour drained from Ms Oleander's face. "Now, really," she said. "You're not seriously going to take the word of a bunch of kids?"

Catherine's mouth twitched. "We will, of course, investigate the claims that Freya and her friends have made. For now it seems only appropriate to place the sale of the boardwalk on hold. I'm certainly not comfortable doing any kind of business with someone who would raise their hand to a young boy. Do you agree, Mr Mayor?"

She turned to glare at the mayor, who was fidgeting helplessly behind her. His face had turned entirely pink. He nodded. Catherine turned back to Ms Oleander with a sickly-sweet smile. "And in the meantime, I'd suggest you find somewhere else to stay."

Mei leapt back on to the plinth, a grin lighting her face. "Get out of our town!" she chanted. "Get out of our town!"

The crowd took up the chant with great enthusiasm, fists punching the beat into the air, banners swinging wildly. Ms Oleander fled through the crowd, flinching away from the words being hurled at her. Lin took Teddy's hands in hers and hoisted him back to his feet. Freya rushed to where his tiara had fallen, brushed it off and plonked it back on his head at a jaunty angle.

"At least she didn't hit my other cheek," said Teddy, rolling his jaw.

"True," said Lin, grabbing him and turning him one way then the other. "They match now."

"You've never looked better," grinned Freya.

Twenty-Five

The entire town turned out to watch as a team of archaeologists brought the treasure out through the tunnel in wheelbarrows. The barrows were tipped out in the little room at the top of the tunnel and sent back down to be refilled. The treasure was carried to the town hall in bags, buckets, basins and bowls under the careful supervision of the archaeologists. Well, careful-ish. Freya was sure some of the treasure disappeared into pockets on the way, but it didn't matter. There was more than enough to go around.

The mayor had slunk into the town hall after the

scene with Ms Oleander and no one had seen much of him since. Catherine had stepped up and was enthusiastically directing the operation. A shimmer round her neck caught Freya's attention and for a moment Freya thought she'd been digging into the treasure herself. Then she realised Catherine was wearing the mayor's gold chain.

Freya pushed through the crowd towards her. "Thank you," she said. "You saved my home."

Catherine laughed and shook her head. "I did nothing of the sort. You saved your home, Freya. You might just have saved the whole town."

Freya shoved her hands into her pockets and wriggled happily.

"You know," said Catherine, "we're going to need a plan for what to do with all of this."

Something inside Freya gave a leap. She looked down into the crowd, where Lin and Mei were playfighting. Or maybe they were actually fighting. It was hard to tell sometimes.

"I think I know some people who might be able to help you with that."

The day became a party without anyone really noticing. The barrows of treasure were replaced with impromptu stalls, rickety tables, makeshift stages. People spilled from the streets down on to the beach and stretched out on the sand, some brave enough to dip their toes in the freezing sea. It felt as though summer had arrived early in Edge, everyone collectively deciding to ignore the slicing sharpness of the breeze, as the sun dropped fast towards the horizon.

Freya found Lin standing on the water's edge, looking out to sea.

"I hope you're not on the lookout for another adventure," said Freya.

Lin laughed. "No, I think I'm ready to be boring for a little while."

Freya squeezed her. "You've never been boring for a second."

Lin gave her a nudge. "I can't believe how brave you were, standing up and speaking out like that. In front of the whole town!"

"I can't really believe it either. I'm not sure where

the courage came from."

"Probably from wearing that tiara," said Lin thoughtfully. "Everyone feels important when they're wearing a tiara."

Freya laughed. "You're supposed to say that the courage was inside me all along. Besides, I think you'll find that it was Teddy wearing the tiara, not me."

Lin grinned. "How could I forget? Where is he anyway? I haven't seen him all day."

Freya frowned. "Neither have I. I hope he hasn't made a run for it."

"I doubt it," said Lin. "Not without his share of the treasure. Did you really promise he could keep half?"

Freya nodded. "I never wanted the treasure for me. Just for the town."

"That's very noble of you," said Lin. She paused. "I could really have done with a new TV, though."

Freya snorted and shoved her. She shivered as a breeze rippled off the sea, ruffling her hair.

Lin produced a flask from her coat and waved it in Freya's direction.

"Magic soup?" asked Freya.

"What else?"

Freya linked an arm through Lin's as she took a sip of the hot soup. She looked out at the choppy waves. She felt as though the cold couldn't touch her now.

It was almost fully dark by the time Freya made her way back to the B&B, her journey punctuated by the glow of bonfires on the sand below. The B&B was quiet, Granny Kate still out enjoying the revelry. The last time Freya had seen her, she was talking animatedly to Ms Hanan, pretending not to have one eye on Harpreet's grandpa, who was pretending not to be making a beeline for her.

Freya made her way up the stairs to Room Three and pushed the door open. It was empty. There was no sign of Ms Oleander at all, nothing to say she'd ever been there, other than the cloying smell of violets hanging in the air. She walked to the window and looked out at the bonfires on the beach. From here, they looked like constellations.

"Hey," came a voice from behind her.

Freya turned. Teddy was leaning against the door frame. Freya gave him a smile. "Hey. Some day. I can't believe how much treasure they found. Have you decided what you're going to do with your half?"

Teddy dropped his gaze. "I spoke to the mayor about that. The new mayor, I mean."

Freya nodded. "I don't think you have to worry about her. She won't keep your share."

"I know. That's what I was speaking to her about. I thought that maybe … maybe we could all just share it."

Freya's eyebrows almost disappeared into her hair. "Share it?"

"Yeah, you know. Half for the town, half for the people in the town. Who really needs more than a handful of treasure anyway?"

Freya beamed at him. "That's amazing, Teddy."

Teddy shrugged. "Whatever."

He turned to leave but stopped at the door. "Your granny has asked me to stick around. If that's all right with you."

Freya grinned and leaned back against the windowsill.

Teddy's eyes filled and he cleared his throat

roughly. He gave a tiny smile and walked away without waiting for Freya to answer.

Freya's head still felt like it was spinning and she rested her forehead against the cool glass. It fogged under her warm skin and she doodled out the beginnings of a new invention with one fingertip. The flowery scent of Ms Oleander's perfume tickled her nose. Freya heaved open the window and took a big breath, letting the salty sea air carry the remnants of her away.

Acknowledgements

Thank you most of all to my big, mad family, who have always been my greatest champions. Mum, Dad, Karla, Colin, Sophie, Kiera, Chris, Jenni, Ross, Hannah, Ella, Granny Rosie, Grampa Dougie, Kathleen, Grandad and all of the Usual Suspects: I love you so much.

Thank you to Dearg the cat and Faolán the dog, without whom this book would have been finished much faster. Thank you to our beautiful Juno, who was the very best girl with the very softest ears.

Thank you to Eddie Bowers, the first person to read an outline of Freya's Gold and tell me to go for it. Thank you to Hux and to my NaNoWriMates, Georgia, Becki, Liv, Chelle, Elena and Cookie, who dealt with so much of my nonsense while I was writing. I may not have survived without the memes.

Thank you to Fiona Scoble, who gently guided this book through the dark and twisting tunnels from a scribbled outline to the story it became. Thank you to my cover illustrator Carmi Grau, and the team at Nosy Crow for creating such a gorgeous book for my story to live in.

Thank you to Julia Silk, who never makes me feel silly, even when I'm being silly.

Thank you to the Irish Arts Council, Monaghan County Council, the Tyrone Guthrie Centre and the incomparable Monaghan Libraries for their support of my writing, and of all artists.

Thank you to every reader, and to every little writer who has come to my creative writing workshops. Helping you tell your stories is the absolute honour of my life.

Thank you always to Niall, who became my husband since the last time I wrote one of these, and who remains my very best friend. Grá mo chroí.